"Drop your we~~~~~~~~~~~~~~ up!"

The assailant spun and fired two rounds through the window.

Dylan ducked out of the way, feeling the rain of broken glass spray across his back and neck. The creep turned and wildly fired three more rounds in Dylan's direction before disappearing into the hallway.

"You okay?" Dylan called to the woman through the broken window. He could see only part of her unmoving body. She didn't respond.

When she gazed up at him, he suddenly realized where he knew her from. She was a 911 emergency dispatcher.

"Hey, Clare, are you all right?"

She looked down at herself. "I think a bullet hit the top of my shoulder. Burns a little, but it doesn't hurt very much."

When she looked back at him, tears rolled down her cheeks and Dylan's heart clenched.

"What happened?" he asked, while listening to the patrol cars pulling up outside. "Who is that guy?"

"I don't know who he is." Her answer came out sounding like a wail. "But he may have murdered my stepmother."

Jenna Night comes from a family of Southern-born natural storytellers. Her parents were avid readers and the house was always filled with books. No wonder she grew up wanting to tell her own stories. She's lived on both coasts but currently resides in the Inland Northwest, where she's astonished by the occasional glimpse of a moose, a herd of elk or a soaring eagle.

Visit the Author Profile page at LoveInspired.com for more titles.

UNSOLVED
MONTANA
INVESTIGATION

JENNA NIGHT

LOVE INSPIRED SUSPENSE
INSPIRATIONAL ROMANCE

LOVE INSPIRED® SUSPENSE
INSPIRATIONAL ROMANCE

ISBN-13: 978-1-335-98057-1

Unsolved Montana Investigation

Love Inspired
22 Adelaide St. West, 41st Floor
Toronto, Ontario M5H 4E3, Canada
www.LoveInspired.com

Printed in U.S.A.

Our soul waiteth for the Lord:
he is our help and our shield.
—*Psalm* 33:20

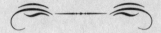

To my mother, Esther, who taught me to love books.

ONE

"This is where it happened," Clare Barlow said softly, even though there was no one else around to hear.

She took a deep breath, exhaled, and reminded herself that the lingering ache in her heart three years after the unsolved murder of her beloved stepmother was a reminder of how blessed she'd been to have Jessica Barlow in her life. Jessica had been Clare's *mother* in every meaningful sense of the word.

A cold, sharp breeze sliced through Garnet Park, ruffling the surrounding tree branches. Clare hugged herself. Spring had made an initial appearance three weeks ago with bright blue skies and mild temperatures. But in Cedar Lodge, Montana, things could change in an instant.

Life could end in an instant, too. Jessica had come to this small city park at the edge of town for reasons unknown and been shot twice, her body discovered near the creek at the base of an oak tree three years ago.

Clare hadn't been able to bring herself to visit this spot before today. But a recent discovery had given her a sense of determination that had previously been overshadowed by grief. Jessica's neck scarf with an attached work ID had been found tangled under a juniper bush close to her place of employment by landscaping workers. The scarf had been brought to the attention of the police and that was when Clare had been shocked to learn her stepmother's murder was officially deemed a cold case. And it would stay that way, it seemed, because according to the police the scarf didn't offer any new actionable information. Clare's proximity to law enforcement through her work as an emergency dispatcher had not helped with the situation.

She should probably have expected the cold case designation. There were no witnesses to the murder, no known motive and no substantial physical evidence. Still, she'd imagined the police were continuing to actively look for the killer. After she learned they weren't, she'd taken to posting on social media, given an interview to the host of a popular cold case podcast, and shown up at a city council meeting requesting that the members get the investigation rebooted.

At the same time she'd felt a responsibility to do whatever she could to uncover evidence or information that might help. It had seemed reasonable to begin her concentrated efforts here, *ground zero* as she thought of it, to get her bearings and think about what she could do next to find some answers.

Clare glanced away from the spot at the base of the tree where her stepmother's body had been found and startled at the unexpected sight of a man, medium height with dark brown eyes, standing a few feet away. Where had he come from?

As an emergency dispatcher, Clare had experience keeping a cool head in a dangerous situation. Even so, her heart lurched in her chest and she felt frozen in place.

"Hard to let go of her after she was gone," the man said quietly. "But you *should* have. You're trying to stir things up with the cops and get them to take a closer look at what happened to Jessica and we don't want that." He lifted the pistol in his hand, pointed it at Clare and fired.

In the instant before he squeezed the trigger Clare managed to turn her body sideways, narrowing her profile so the bullet flew by. She stumbled backward until she was behind a cluster of trees, fear rushing through her veins and triggering a ripple of goose bumps across her skin.

What is happening?

Someone was trying to kill her, that's what. Just like they'd killed Jessica.

"Don't make this difficult for me and I'll make it quick and painless for you," the man called out.

Dear Lord, help!

Still hidden behind the pine trees, frozen in fear, Clare heard the man's footsteps crunch atop the pine cones and dried needles as he strode toward her.

Bang!

The bullet from the second shot tore off a strip of tree bark and splinters struck Clare's face. A bracing slap of stark terror snapped her out of inaction and set her running in a zigzag pattern with no specific goal other than getting away, hoping the trees and boulders would make her a more difficult target as she raced between them.

Bang!

This bullet hit a boulder a foot in front of her, pinging as it sent up a puff of pulverized rock and then ricocheted off into the forest. Clare heard pounding footsteps behind her. The shooter was closing in. The next shot might find its mark.

Panic clouded Clare's thinking as her heart hammered in her chest. She tried to form some kind of plan. Continuing to run through the woods, hoping to get away from the shooter, wasn't going to be enough. Her lungs burned as she gasped for air and ran across the grassy, uneven ground.

Her car, that was where she needed to go. Even if the process of getting to it would force her out into the open, where it would be easier for the gunman to see her. If she could reach the parking lot and her car, at least she would have a chance of getting away. She made a sudden, sharp change in direction. After a few steps she realized she didn't hear the gunman behind her. Maybe she'd thrown him off long enough to escape.

She shoved her hand into her pocket and reassured herself that her key fob was still there. She felt a sudden firm tug on her arm and whirled around expecting to face the shooter. Instead, she realized a tree branch had snagged the strap of her shoulder bag and pulled it off her body. She tried to quickly find it in the brush under the tree, but searching was taking too long and the shooter was still after her. She had to leave it behind. She darted from the cover of the trees in the park and ran across the sidewalk to the parking lot.

Her car was the only vehicle in the lot—no surprise since it was a weekday morning and she hadn't seen anyone in the park other than the gunman. Fortunately, her sedan wasn't far away. She jammed her hand into her pocket, pressed the button on the fob and heard the reassuring chirp as her doors unlocked.

She reached for the handle on the driver's-side door and heard another gunshot. A bullet punched a hole in the backseat side window, mere inches from her head. The perp was catching up with her. If she got into the car now, he'd just shoot her though the glass.

Unable to think of a better option, she sprinted toward

the road that ran by the park's entrance, hoping that someone driving by would stop to help her.

A sedan approached as she neared the road and she waved her arms as best she could while running, certain that the sight of a man chasing a fleeing woman across a parking lot would tell the driver all they needed to know.

Bang!

This shot fired by her pursuer tore through her right sleeve and burned the skin at the top of her shoulder. The shocking reality of getting shot stole her breath and for a moment she couldn't expand her lungs.

Still, she found the strength to kick up her pace and run even harder. She was able to breathe again, though by now her breaths were more like gulps, and sparkles were appearing at the edge of her vision. She was on the verge of passing out.

Racing toward the slowing car on the road, she saw the astonished-looking faces of the man and woman in the front seat. Then she spotted the two small children in the back seat, neither one more than five years old.

The attacker was close behind Clare and she couldn't put these innocent children in danger. She adjusted her trajectory and bolted across the road in front of it. Seconds later she heard brakes squealing and the sound of a thump. Had the car struck something? Had it collided with the attacker?

Clare was too scared to slow down and take a look. Her phone was in the purse she'd been forced to leave behind so she couldn't call for help in case the people in the car had been injured. All she could do was send up a prayer for the occupants of the vehicle, especially the children, and keep running until she collapsed or found a safe place to stop.

The creek she'd been standing near in the park flowed through a large culvert under the road she'd just crossed. If she were to continue in the direction she was going and follow the creek to its source, it would ultimately take her to the snow melting atop a nearby mountain. But she wouldn't need to go that far to find help. Clare had explored Garnet Park and the area around the creek on both sides of the road with her friends when she was a teenager. She knew there were houses and cabins alongside the creek in the direction she was headed. There was bound to be somebody around who would help her or at least call the police.

Running through the thick grass and trees along the bank of the creek, she rounded a bend and came to a rustic cabin she remembered seeing as a kid. It had been neglected in the years since and was obviously uninhabited.

Disappointment dropped heavy on her shoulders. What if she'd made a horrible mistake and she didn't find anyone to help her before the assailant caught up with her?

Clare slowed and finally looked behind her, but the thick forest kept her from seeing very far. Was the attacker closing in on her? The gurgle and splashes of creek water rushing over the rocks and the caws of crows circling overhead made it impossible to hear any subtle sounds. After a moment she thought she did hear something that didn't quite fit with the sounds of nature. Was she hearing the attacker's voice or was she imagining it?

Keep moving.

She resumed running along the bank. Just as she wondered if she'd be better off to step into the cold water and swim across to the other side, she spotted a stone chimney visible through the pines. Glad to avoid going into the water, she rushed toward it. She wove her way through the trees for several yards until her gaze fell upon the back side of a well-kept two-story cabin. Relief poured over her as she raced up the steps to the back door and knocked on it. *"Help!"* she called out, trying not to be too loud in case the gunman was nearby. "I need help. *Please!* Call the police!"

She pressed her face to the window beside a door. It didn't look as if anyone was home.

Maybe whoever lived there was asleep. Terrified that the gun-wielding criminal was closing in on her, Clare knocked again, this time more quietly. "I need help," she repeated with her nose touching the door, hoping that her continued pleas for assistance would not draw the assailant to her. She grabbed the door handle and twisted it. Locked.

She couldn't hear any sounds from inside. Not even a barking dog.

She stepped off the porch and ran around to the front of the cabin. The door there was also locked. She saw a metal carport but no car. At the end of a driveway she could see a section of the rutted dirt drive that would eventually lead back to the paved road she'd previously crossed. But if she ran down that road she'd make herself an easy target for the gunman.

Uncertain what to do and exhausted, Clare pressed her back to the side of the cabin and slid down until she was squatting. Maybe she should wait here and hope the attacker bypassed the cabin and continued along the creek bank. She listened attentively as several seconds ticked by and she didn't hear him.

But then she hadn't heard him when he'd originally approached her in the park. So maybe he was closing in on her without her realizing it.

Nearly sick with fear, she shoved herself to her feet. Staying here in plain sight hoping he wouldn't find her didn't seem like a good idea. What if he found her trail leading up to the cabin from the creek bank and followed it? There were probably people in the cabins and houses dispersed throughout the area, but wandering around searching for someone would just make it easier for the shooter to spot her.

What she needed to do was find a good place to hide until the gunman wandered away from this area as he searched for her.

Getting inside the cabin seemed like the best choice. She glanced around and spotted a metal snow shovel propped against the building near the back door. She grabbed it, and after listening for a moment and not hearing sounds of the assailant, she broke a window as quietly as possible and then quickly cleared the edges.

She pulled over a redwood bench and stepped on it so she could climb inside. Maybe she was being overly optimistic, but it seemed possible she'd find a house phone inside or an unlocked tablet so she could contact the police for help. Or maybe she'd trigger an alarm and the cabin owner would call the cops.

It was also possible that she was only delaying the inevitable and this was the end of the line for her. But she had to at least try.

Deputy Sheriff Dylan Ruiz keyed the mic in his patrol car. "Dispatch, SD-615. Can you confirm caller is *not* in the residence at this time?"

"Confirm, SD-615. Caller reports he is away at work. Home video shows a woman breaking into his residence followed by a male breaking into the residence. The male was brandishing a gun and appeared to be in pursuit of the female."

"Copy," Dylan responded. "Is video of the current situation available?"

"Negative. Caller reports the male assailant spotted the two security cameras inside the home and disconnected them."

"Copy. I'm approximately two minutes out."

Dylan eased off the gas pedal to avoid a tailspin as he turned from the paved highway onto one of the many dirt roads crisscrossing Garnet Hills. He'd already been in the vicinity while responding to a call from a driver who'd reported seeing a woman pursued by an armed assailant before braking too hard to avoid them and then sliding off the road.

Seemed extremely likely the two events were connected.

Since Dylan was the closest responding unit, he'd been redirected to the higher-priority, life-threatening situation. His old friend, Police Officer Kris Volker, had been dispatched to meet with the driver who'd made the original call.

Dylan's patrol car bottomed out a couple of times as he sped over the rises and drops of the dirt and mud-mixed road as it cut a path through the trees. He shot past a scattering of mailboxes on posts along with some gates marking the driveways of the cabins and houses.

Adrenaline ratcheted his heart rate and sent his thoughts racing as he considered multiple scenarios of what he might find when he arrived on scene. Six years in the Marine Corps, including two tours in combat zones, had given Dylan experience in thinking ahead while at the same time being prepared to pivot plans at a moment's notice. Other law enforcement officers would be responding, but he had no intention of waiting for them.

A stealth response seemed wise in this situation, so

he killed his lights and siren. He took his foot off the accelerator as he approached a mailbox with a number on it confirming this was the residence he was looking for.

He keyed his radio mic. "Dispatch, SD-615. Show me on scene."

"Copy."

He turned onto the dirt driveway, moving slowly at first in case the man with the gun was still there and decided to take a shot at him. He didn't want to rush into an ambush. That gave Dylan a few extra seconds to take in the cabin in front of him. It appeared as if it had started out as a simple wooden structure and then had additional rooms added over time. He spotted a narrow front door with a broken window beside it. There was a metal carport on the other side of a patch of scraggly grass. So far, he didn't see anyone or any sign of movement.

Lord, please guide me.

He got out of the car and strode forward, gun in hand. He moved quickly through the shadows offered by the pine trees until he approached a window on the back of the cabin where he could look inside.

A woman's scream snared his attention before he could see anything. More screams followed. Rather than forcing the door open and rushing into an unknown situation, he moved to the edge of the window and then leaned over to get a glimpse of what was happening.

He saw an open floor plan with a living room, dining area and part of a kitchen. He also saw the bottom of a staircase. Every cabinet door in sight was flung open, including one at the base of the staircase. In front of that door stood a man, with a woman at his feet. He clenched a fistful of her dark blond hair in one hand. In his other hand he held a gun. The woman fought him as he pulled her away from the storage cabinet where she must have been hiding.

As the woman twisted and kicked, the gunman lifted his gun and pointed it at her.

He's going to shoot her!

Dylan kicked the door open. "Drop your weapon!"

The gunman yanked the woman to her feet, then let go of her hair to pull her in front of himself and use her as a shield.

"I said *drop your weapon*!" Dylan commanded again, keeping his eye on the perp's gun

The attacker turned to Dylan. "Back off or I'll kill her!"

The woman froze. She lifted her head and locked gazes with Dylan.

I know you. He didn't know why she looked familiar, but he could figure that out later.

Bang!

The criminal fired off a shot, sending a spray of splinters from the doorframe onto the back porch as Dylan darted out of the way.

"You don't have to do this!" Dylan yelled from the back porch. There was no telling what the gunman's endgame was. Maybe he was high and delusional. Maybe the woman was his wife and she'd told him she wanted a divorce and this was intended to be a murder-suicide.

Hostage negotiation wasn't Dylan's strong suit. He was wired for action. "Put down your gun! We can work this out!"

Without waiting for an answer, he took another look inside but didn't see the woman or the attacker. He heard footsteps and scraping sounds coming from a hallway. Stepping inside, he caught a flash of movement just before the attacker dragged the woman into a room and slammed the door shut. Maybe he was afraid that if he shot the woman in front of Dylan, Dylan would shoot *him*.

What was this jerk's plan? Why would he corner himself in the cabin with a cop at the door? Maybe he really did intend to kill the woman and himself.

Or to kill the woman and escape through a window.

Racing down the hallway toward the closed door on wooden floors would only announce to the attacker that the deputy was coming and possibly goad the criminal into shooting the woman.

So Dylan backed out and ran around the outside of the cabin to the front. He looked into a window in the area where the gunman was holed up and saw that it was a bedroom. The assailant clutched the woman's arm while staring at the closed door, as if trying to determine whether Dylan was headed down the hallway toward him.

The assailant shifted his weight from side to side, obviously agitated. Maybe he was weighing his options, but his actions indicated he didn't want to negotiate and Dylan was afraid the criminal would shoot his hostage at any moment. The deputy didn't want to fire through the window and risk hitting the woman. He was considering his next move when the woman wobbled on her feet, appearing about to collapse. Stumbling, she turned her head as she regained her balance and saw Dylan. He held his finger to his lips for her to stay quiet and hoped she wouldn't visibly react.

Fortunately, the gunman was still focused on the door. Dylan would use that against him. *Please, Lord, let this work.*

Still holding the woman's gaze, Dylan cupped his ear, then put his hand beside his mouth as if yelling, and then pointed at the door before pointing at himself.

She stared at him uncomprehendingly.

He did it again, mouthing the words, *Pretend you hear me*.

Remarkably, after a moment, she appeared to understand. She turned back toward the bedroom door and through the window Dylan heard her shout, "He's coming to the door! That cop is coming! We're going to get shot!"

The criminal took a wide stance and used both hands to aim and steady his gun.

The woman stumbled toward the window and Dylan gestured for her to get down before yelling, "Drop your weapon and put your hands up!"

The assailant spun and fired two rounds through the window.

Dylan ducked out of the way, feeling the rain of broken glass spray across his back and neck. He stood in time to see the criminal yank open the door. Before Dylan could shoot back, the man turned and wildly fired three more rounds in Dylan's direction before disappearing into the hallway.

"You okay?" Dylan called to the woman through the broken window. He could only see part of her unmoving body. She didn't respond.

He ran to the back of the house yet again. Trampled wild grass and swaying pine branches made it obvious the creep had fled toward the creek.

Instinct screamed at Dylan to chase after the shooter. But his stronger moral compass demanded he go back to check on the woman and render first aid if necessary.

He entered the cabin and found the woman sitting on the floor by the window, rubbing a red area on her arm where the assailant had held on to her.

Dylan squatted beside her. When she gazed up at him,

he suddenly realized where he knew her from. She was a 911 emergency dispatcher.

Clare.

"Hey, Clare, are you all right?"

"I think so." Her voice shook.

Wailing emergency sirens drew near. Dylan keyed his collar mic to update the responders and give a description of the gunman who was now at large.

"You sure you didn't take a bullet anywhere?" Dylan asked Clare gently. He sat on the floor beside her. "Sometimes you don't feel it until the adrenaline drops."

She looked down at herself. "I think a bullet hit the top of my shoulder and scraped off a layer of skin. Burns a little but it doesn't hurt very much. I don't see any blood seeping through my jacket."

When she looked back at him, fat tears rolled down her cheeks, and Dylan's heart clenched. He would feel empathy with anybody in this situation, but he felt especially bad that it was Clare. How many times had she assisted someone desperately calling in an emergency? And how many times had she been the calm and strengthening voice Dylan heard over the radio in the midst of a volatile situation? He didn't see her often but he heard her nearly every day.

"What happened?" he asked, while hearing patrol cars pull up outside along with an EMS crew. "Who is that guy?"

"I don't know" Her answer came out sounding like a wail. "But he may have murdered my stepmother."

That's right, her stepmother, Jessica. He remembered the murder from three years ago and that the case had remained unsolved. Now some creep, possibly the same creep, intended to kill Clare and thought he'd get away with this murder, too?

Not on Dylan's watch.

TWO

"I can give you a ride to the hospital to get checked out," paramedic Cole Webb said to Clare as they sat in the cabin's living room where barely a half hour ago she'd feared for her life. "Don't know if you're aware of it, but Huckleberry Delights opened a bakery and coffee shop across the street from the emergency department. You could head over there after a doctor gives you the all clear. Would make it worth the trip."

Clare smiled faintly in response. They knew each other through work.

"I'll buy you a huckleberry lemonade if you see the doc," Dylan Ruiz added, his voice tight and his stance tense.

"Huh," Cole said quietly, his gaze shifting to Dylan and resting there before raising an eyebrow. Dylan glared at him and after a moment Cole turned back to Clare with a faint smile on his face.

Clare had no idea what that little exchange meant, but she knew Dylan, Cole and Cedar Lodge Police Officer Kris Volker had all been friends since they were kids. They'd played high school football together, along with their friend Henry Walsh, and after that they'd gone off to serve in the military. Dylan, Cole and Kris had all returned to northern Montana to pursue careers in public safety and it was common for them to cross paths as they served the community. What their friend Henry had gone on to do was a bit of a mystery to her.

"The spot where the bullet grazed my shoulder is a little sore, but it's not a significant injury," Clare said to Cole. She turned back to Dylan. "I'm fine. Really."

Dylan nodded. "Okay."

Cole packed up his gear and gave Clare's hand a light squeeze. "I'm sorry this happened to you," he said before heading out.

Dylan had his radio turned up and both he and Clare listened to the communications traffic for a moment. It was strange for Clare to hear her coworkers at the dispatch center talking about a situation she was involved in. It was also unsettling to listen to the various law enforcement officers she knew who were searching Garnet Park and the bank along the creek where the gunman had pursued her.

"There's a sedan in the lot at Garnet Park with the driver-side rear window shot out." Clare recognized Officer Volker's voice. "Standby for a plate number and registration check."

"That's my car," Clare said quietly.

Dylan relayed the message.

"A handbag was found in the brush nearby," Volker added. "I checked the wallet for ID and it looks like it belongs to Clare. There's a phone in here, too."

Thank You, Lord. In the scheme of things, her purse and everything in it were inconsequential, but recovering them would make her life a little easier.

More voices came across Dylan's radio—officers reporting on their search area as they looked for the attacker and each one stating that they hadn't picked up the man's trail beyond the point where he'd apparently gone into the creek. The K-9 handler had been dispatched, but she hadn't arrived yet. If the assailant was hiding nearby the dog would find him. If the creep had returned to an as-yet undiscovered vehicle and driven away or been picked up by an accomplice, that would bring an abrupt end to the search.

A two-person forensic team arrived accompanied by the sergeant from the sheriff's department who'd been among the first responders. Dylan had already explained to Clare that Sergeant Tate Reid would be in charge of the scene and would help in the investigation. Following a brief conversation with the forensic team, the sergeant went back outside.

One of the techs asked for a summary of what had happened and then asked if they could borrow Clare's coat to see if they could find any evidence on it. "Since he held on to you, there's a chance he might have left a hair behind or a fiber from clothes that we'd be able to match to him at a later date should he be captured."

Clare handed over her coat. Wouldn't it be something if this was how they ended up finding her stepmother's killer?

"It's my house! I have a right to go in there!" a male stated emphatically outside the front door. "I'm the one who called *you*!"

The cabin owner.

Clare got to her feet.

"Sir, this is a crime scene," a cop-like voice replied.

"I want to talk to him." Clare trudged to the door, her steps feeling heavy following the most intense physical workout she'd had in ages. Dylan stayed close beside her.

"You're alive!" the man called out when she reached

the doorway. "I saw you on my video feed and I saw that maniac going after you before he unplugged the cameras. I called the cops and I prayed the whole drive over that you'd be okay!"

"You saved my life," Clare said, and then she burst into tears. Her response seemed to come from nowhere, as without warning she began sobbing and had trouble catching her breath.

From beside her Dylan wrapped a muscled arm around her shoulders. And then after a moment he turned until he had both arms around her and she pressed her face into his chest, aware that she was soaking his crisp black uniform shirt with her tears, but she just couldn't stop.

"Breathe," Dylan said quietly.

After a couple of failed attempts, she was able to take a deep breath. And then another. After that she was finally able to assert a modicum of control over herself, slow her sobbing, and then take a step back from the deputy. She wiped her eyes and tried not to look at him. She was normally a person with self-control. She had to stay calm as a dispatcher and she prided herself on being able to do that no matter how intense the pressure. Deputy Dylan Ruiz wasn't exactly a coworker in the sense of her being physically around him most work days. But they were colleagues, and this was not how she wanted to present herself with him or any of the other law enforcement officers.

Especially not after the gossip and criticism that had led to her current leave of absence from work, which had begun six weeks after the discovery of her late stepmother's scarf. There were already enough people who thought her determination to personally find evidence that would lead to her stepmother's killer was a sign that she wasn't thinking clearly.

Clare squared her shoulders, turned and walked toward the slender, balding, middle-aged man standing at the doorway, his face red with agitation.

"Thanks to you, I'm alive," Clare said to him. She glanced around and pressed her lips together in an apologetic smile. "There's some damage to your house, I'm afraid. But I'll pay for it."

The man shook his head. "Let me talk to my insurance agent first. I'm just grateful you're all right." His eyes widened slightly. "And I sure hope that criminal doesn't come back."

As they exchanged names and contact information, Clare was aware of Dylan taking a phone call. When her conversation with the cabin owner concluded, Dylan walked over to her. She grimaced inwardly at the spot on his shirt that she dampened when she was crying. Then she forced herself to look up into his dark brown eyes. He was a handsome man. Military-cut black hair, warm tan skin, and typically sporting an intense expression that made it all the more touching when he smiled.

While she'd spoken to him a lot on the radio, she hadn't spent much time with him in person. And she didn't remember ever having the awkward, overly self-aware feeling she was experiencing now. But she would get past this new *interested* feeling, because she had to. He was a law enforcement officer and she knew how dangerous that job was. After having lost her stepmother to a violent attack, there was no way she would risk experiencing the same trauma by letting herself get too close to a cop. Besides, the focus of her life right now was finding Jessica's killer. She had no time for romantic relationships. She took a breath and squared her shoulders, determined to settle her emotions and shift her thoughts away from the deputy.

"Sheriff Finley would like you and me to meet with her in her office right now. Are you up to it?"

"Of course." The words came out sounding snippy, which was not her intention. But at the same time, she didn't want Deputy Dylan Ruiz or anybody else thinking of her as weak.

"Let's go," she added, making her tone sound more agreeable. She walked out the front door ahead of Dylan, then hesitated, waiting to see which patrol car she was supposed to ride in. Her gaze swept across the yard and toward the nearby tree-covered hills. Even with cops around her, she felt nervous. That creep was still out there. Maybe watching right now.

She'd wanted to drum up attention for her stepmother's cold case murder. It looked like she'd done that and then some.

Dylan turned on the heater in his patrol car. Clare was in the seat beside him, her arms crossed, obviously cold. He'd offered her his jacket, but she'd declined.

"It's likely you'll be asked to repeat your description of what happened to you several times over the next few days," Dylan said, with yet another glance at Clare. "I'm sure the sheriff is going to ask for a rundown when we get to the station."

"Whatever it takes," Clare responded.

They were headed down the dirt road leading out of Garnet Hills and back to the paved road. Clare continually looked around, just like Dylan did. The attacker could be nearby. They weren't far from the park. The gunman might have stashed his car on one of these rustic roads, where it would be out of sight, before following Clare into the park. That would explain why she'd seen no vehicle other than her own in the parking lot.

They reached the intersection with the paved road. Clare's sedan was visible in the parking lot with crime scene tape around it. A couple of city police officers were walking in the park, looking for physical evidence tied to the initial attack. Dylan realized Clare was probably anxious to recover her purse and phone, but he wanted to get her to the sheriff's department as quickly as possible. And he didn't want her back in that parking lot until he was certain it was secure.

"I'll get you to your car, or to your home, or anywhere else you want to go after we talk to the sheriff."

"Thank you."

"Is there somebody you need to call?" he asked. "You can use my phone." Dylan had been by her side since the attacker fled and she hadn't phoned anyone. He found that unusual, so he was curious. And yeah, maybe he wanted to know if she was married. Not for any particular reason. Actually, it might be better if he didn't know. He had a career change in the works and had an actual job offer on the table. He needed something more challenging and dangerous than being a small-town deputy. Something that would offer more opportunities to put that surge of excitement he was missing back into his life. Maybe something like what had just happened at the cabin, but on a more regular basis. Typically, his work shifts were much quieter than this.

"I want to wait to tell my dad about this until he can see for himself that I'm okay." Clare ran a hand through her shoulder-length, dark blond hair before dropping it back into her lap. "This is going to hit close to home for him."

Pretty much everyone who had lived in town when it

happened knew about the murder of Jessica Barlow. But asking anything about that right now, while Clare was understandably still rattled, seemed cruel.

At the same time, not asking questions about the crime that had happened *today* would be a dereliction on his part.

"You notice anybody following you while you were driving in town today?" Dylan asked. He hadn't pursued a higher rank in the department because he didn't want to spend a lot of time behind a desk. He preferred action and that was what he got working patrol. Nevertheless, his military experience had taught him solid investigative skills and he would do everything he could to unravel today's events and track down the criminal who'd tried to kill Clare. Fortunately, Sheriff Finley appreciated his abilities and sometimes allowed him to help with investigations.

"You figure that's how the creep found me at the park?" Clare turned to Dylan. "You think the attacker saw me in town this morning while I was getting coffee and running errands and he followed me to the scene of the crime where my stepmother was found?" There was a brief hesitation before she added more slowly, "Or maybe he knows where I live and he followed me from my apartment."

"Unless you told someone you were going to the park today, the possibility of him finding you earlier and then following you makes the most sense." If the assailant knew where she lived, he would have just killed her while she was home.

"I didn't tell anybody where I was going today. I didn't notice anyone following me, either. I wasn't watching for that, but obviously I should have been."

"Why would you be watching?"

"*Seriously?* You're going to pretend you don't know?"

"I don't have to pretend," Dylan said evenly. "Tell me what I obviously don't know."

She didn't answer right away, so he glanced over and saw her giving him an assessing look.

"You don't spend much time on local news sites or social media?" she finally asked.

"No. I work as a deputy sheriff. I help out on my parents' ranch. I catch a few of the major news headlines when I'm checking the weather, but otherwise I don't spend a lot of time online."

She uncrossed her arms. The patrol car had gotten warmer, and hopefully, she was feeling more comfortable.

"You may or may not have noticed that I haven't been working dispatch for the last few days," she finally said.

"You've been taking some time off?"

"I was strongly encouraged to." She exhaled a breath through her nose. "Are you *sure* you haven't heard the gossip?"

"Just tell me."

"Fine. My stepmother's neck scarf, with her work ID still attached, was found downtown last month by workers outside a business that was updating its landscaping and driveway." The words came out very quickly and she became more animated, gesturing with her hands as she spoke.

Dylan could see the strength of her emotions coming to the surface and empathy for what she must have gone through following the murder of her stepmother brought a lump to his throat.

"I thought the discovery of the scarf would trigger some kind of action by the police department regarding my stepmother's case. It didn't, beyond them accepting the item, doing a forensic check that told them nothing, and then cataloging it."

"I'm sorry that happened to you," Dylan said quietly. If it had been him working the case, he would have considered the feelings of the family, and at the very least he would have met with them to address their concerns.

"At that point I learned that her murder investigation had officially become a cold case a few months earlier," Clare continued. "I didn't know that. Nobody had notified us."

Dylan sighed audibly, doing his best to keep the anger he felt on her behalf over this insensitive treatment of Clare and her family under control. "That's inexcusable. Someone should have told you about that before then."

Clare nodded. "When I spoke with the lead detective on the original case, Detective Anthony Graham, he said finding the scarf wasn't reason enough to reopen the case. It didn't offer any helpful clues. That they still had no motive, no witnesses and no evidence that would move the case forward."

"I wish none of this had happened to you," Dylan said. His line of work often put him in contact with good people who'd just been through a horrible experience. The helpless feeling of being unable to change the situation tugged at his heart every time. "This is not meant as an excuse, but sometimes cops get so caught up in the facts of a crime that they forget to consider the feelings of the people involved." He cleared his throat. Talking about feelings was not something he was good at, but for Clare's sake he would give it a try. "I know you truly loved your stepmother, and you don't want her to be forgotten."

"You're right, I don't want that to happen. I won't let it." Her voice broke and she began to sniff.

Dylan reached into the console to grab a box of tissues and offer them to her.

She pulled out a few of them. "Thanks." She sniffed a couple more times and then cleared her throat. "I talked to Chief Ellis about it, and he agreed with what the detective told me. He also threw in the same excuse we hear so often about how the increase in the population of Cedar Lodge over the last few years has stretched resources thin and how tax revenue hasn't caught up with costs yet."

"I'm sorry," Dylan said. He probably sounded like a broken record, but he could live with that. Someone from law enforcement should apologize for how coldly Clare had been treated. He was willing to be the one to do that.

"Yeah, well, I wasn't sorry. I was mad. So I started my own investigation. I figured I'd piece together a timeline of what my stepmother, Jessica, had been doing the day she was murdered along with the week ahead of that. I wanted to find out where people had seen her and who they'd seen her with. Talk to her friends and coworkers. Stuff like that. I posted some questions and statements on social media to nudge things along and see if anyone remembered anything. I talked to the local online newspaper and they published an interview. I talked to a true crime podcaster with a wide national audience and that's when I *really* got into trouble."

"Trouble?" Dylan glanced at her with his eyebrows raised.

"It made Detective Graham angry. He thought I was making him look bad. The mayor and some of the city council members thought it made them look bad, too. The controversy worked its way through to emergency services and ultimately to my boss. I was told I was maligning the police department and undermining public trust in city government and I needed to stop."

"But you didn't?" Dylan had some experience working with bureaucrats and administrators who were more concerned with good appearances than a job correctly done, and he understood her frustration.

Clare sighed. "Around the same time, on two different occasions, I came out from my apartment to find a note on my car telling me to stop what I was doing and be grateful that nothing bad had happened to me—yet."

A flare of concern prompted Dylan to sit up straighter. "You reported that to the police, I hope." He already knew Clare was in danger because of today's attack, but it appeared that the situation was worse than he'd thought.

"I did contact the police. But the only fingerprints they found on the notes were mine and there were no nearby security cameras to capture images of the person putting them in place. Then the rumors started that I had put the letters there myself to get the cops to reopen my step-mom's case." She cleared her throat. "I suppose I convinced myself that the notes were written by some mean prankster and I didn't take them as serious threats."

"And you left your job?" Dylan prompted. As if the threat to Clare's life wasn't enough, it was now clear that law enforcement and much of the town's justice and emergency services systems had let her down, and the thought of that made Dylan's stomach turn.

"My supervisor was being pressured, but instead of firing me she offered me an unpaid two-week leave of absence to 'pull myself together' as she put it. So I have fourteen days to conduct an investigation since no one else is doing it. If I go beyond that timeline, then I'll probably lose my job."

He understood her concern. He knew she was a good emergency dispatcher and she seemed to enjoy it. But for the sake of her own safety, Dylan hoped today's events would put an end to her investigation and that she would take her time off to rest and recover from what she'd been through before returning to work.

Listening to the strength in her voice and determination in her tone, though, he doubted she would do that. He was afraid for what might happen to her as she tried to investigate a murder case on her own.

"Who's helping you with this?" he asked. "Your dad, maybe?"

She shook her head. "I have a fifteen-year-old brother, Steve. Half brother, legally. But he's my *brother*. Our dad's concerned about Steve's safety and didn't want to get involved because he was worried about something happening to me or my brother like the attack today." She looked over at Dylan. "I'm okay with Dad's decision. I'll do what I can to keep him and Steve out of this. But I'm not going to quit."

Dylan didn't like the idea of her continuing to search for answers on her own. That would be too dangerous.

They arrived at the sheriff's department and he made the turn into the parking lot.

"I wanted to stir up an investigation," Clare said as they pulled into a slot. "But I didn't imagine it would happen like this."

"I know you want justice for your stepmother," Dylan said as they got out of the truck. He glanced around for anything that looked suspicious as he moved closer to her. "But right now we need to focus on *you* and keeping you safe while we search for the criminal who attacked you because he also just might be your stepmother's killer."

In his years of public service, Dylan had seen selfless people seriously hurt or killed working alone while trying to uncover the details behind criminal activities. He didn't want that to happen to Clare. Fortunately, as a deputy sheriff, he was in a position to help her and he believed he should. Hopefully, the sheriff would be in agreement.

THREE

"Please, take a seat." Sheriff Belinda Finley offered Clare a sympathetic smile and gestured toward the visitor chairs in front of her desk.

Dylan had led the way to his boss's office and made the introductions, and now sat down beside Clare. When he glanced over at her, Clare felt a ripple of warm reassurance in the midst of her still-churning emotions.

"Can I get you a bottle of water or some coffee?" the sheriff asked.

"No, thank you." The fear and dread that had wrapped itself around Clare when she was being pursued along the creek bank had caught up with her again and her stomach felt unsettled. Being here brought back memories of visits to the city police department following the discovery of Jessica's body in the park. The offices and uniforms here at the sheriff's department looked different than at Cedar Lodge PD, but the sounds and the feeling were the same.

Lord, I know You're with me, always. Clare squeezed the cool metal armrests on her chair, anchoring herself in the moment and reminding herself that she was safe. At least for now.

"Tell me what happened." The silver-haired sheriff leaned back in her chair to listen.

Clare began with the startling appearance of the gunman at the park and ended with Dylan rushing to her rescue at the cabin where the assailant had followed her. "The creep said something like '*we*' don't want you stirring things up with the cops," Clare added at the end. "Maybe there was more than one person involved in my stepmother's murder. Or he might have just wanted it to sound that way." It was a detail that had stuck in her mind.

The sheriff scratched out some notes on a yellow legal pad.

"Deputy Ruiz, did the gunman look familiar to you?"

"No, ma'am, he did not."

"Ms. Barlow, have you ever seen the attacker before?"

"No. And please, call me Clare."

The sheriff nodded. "Okay, Clare. Rest assured that while the three of us are sitting here talking, other deputies and members of the police department are actively working on this case. We'll lift images of the perpetrator from the home security video and if the quality is good enough we'll run them through state and federal criminal databases and see if we get a hit."

"Thank you."

"We'll also grab a few mugshots of known local criminals for you to look at as a backup in case the database searches don't work out. The majority of the assault on you and the attempted murder happened in my jurisdiction, so my department will spearhead the investigation." The sheriff locked her steely, blue-eyed gaze on Clare. "I intend to get this creep captured and locked up as quickly as possible."

Clare sighed. The attack was a horrible experience, but at least she had members of law enforcement involved in the case and that made her feel a little bit better. "Good."

"Did the assailant *sound* familiar? Think about it for a moment. Is it possible you've heard his voice before?"

"I don't believe so."

The sheriff nodded. "Okay, let's back this up a little. You've been intent on looking into the murder of Jessica Barlow, your stepmother."

"And having this creep come after me is proof that I'm on to something!" Clare leaned forward in her chair, her heart pounding excitedly. "At the very least, this proves the murderer is somebody local. That the homicide detective's suggestion that Jessica's murder could have been a random hit by some degenerate passing through town was wrong." Clare took a breath and leaned back in her chair. "My stepmother's killer is right here in town. We know that now."

The sheriff lifted an eyebrow. "Maybe. Maybe not. Information posted online goes everywhere. It could draw someone to town who for some incomprehensible reason wanted to connect himself to the murder. Or who suffered from delusions and believed he was already connected. I'm aware that you were interviewed on an online podcast. That could have triggered someone to do this." Finley clasped her hands and set them on her desk. "It's too early to jump to conclusions. Here at the outset, we need to consider as many angles as possible."

"But you've got to admit the threat and attack on Clare today are reason enough to reopen Jessica's murder investigation," Dylan interjected.

Clare turned to him, relieved to have him on her side. Sadly, she'd reached a point where she didn't really expect much help from law enforcement when it came to investigating Jessica's murder case. But Dylan seemed different.

"It's more than reason enough to look into the attempted

murder of *you*," the sheriff said, focusing her attention on Clare. "This attack on its own doesn't bring forth any new evidence or a witness or show a motive for your stepmother's murder. Without those elements there's nothing new to investigate. If in our pursuit of the assailant who attacked you *today* we come across something that could move your stepmother's case forward and prompt police homicide detectives to reopen it, then we will bring it to their attention. But my focus will be on this crime that just happened."

Clare burst into tears before she could stop herself. Despite her cynicism, she'd started to think it possible that today's attack would help get her stepmother's murder case reopened. Now that hope had been crushed.

"You'll notify Clare immediately if you learn anything related to her stepmother's murder, right?" Dylan asked as he grabbed a box of tissues on the sheriff's desk, pulled some out and handed them to Clare.

Sorrow and frustration clogged her throat and she couldn't get out a word of thanks before pressing the tissues to her eyes and nose. It all felt so hopeless now, but she couldn't give up. She *wouldn't* stop trying to get justice for a stepmom who hadn't given up on Clare when she was at her brattiest growing up. A kid angry that her biological mother, Margot, had simply walked away from Clare and her dad. A bitter, ungrateful girl who'd flat-out told Jessica that she didn't want her, she wanted her *real* mom.

Jessica had toughed it out, though. She and Clare's dad had had a son, Clare's brother, Steve. And somewhere in the mix of everything after a few years passed, Clare had realized that Jessica *was* her real mom. A woman who loved her and supported her and cared for her no matter what. She would be forever grateful that she'd come round to tell Jessica how much she loved and appreciated her, before Jessica was so brutally taken from Clare's family.

"Pursuing your own investigation is dangerous and I suggest you stop," the sheriff said after Clare regained her composure.

Clare looked down at the damp tissues in her hand. "I can't do that. Not yet. Maybe not ever." She took a breath and shook her head. "The Cedar Lodge police won't re-open the case because there are no new leads. There aren't any new leads because detectives aren't out looking for them since it's a cold case." She settled her gaze on the sheriff. "I don't think I'm some genius detective who's smarter than everyone else. But I was somewhat familiar with my stepmom's routine. I knew some of her friends and coworkers. Maybe one of them will tell me something they forgot to tell the cops. Maybe someone will tell me about something they saw and didn't realize it could be important."

"You make a good argument," Dylan said. "Obviously, you've thought this through."

A faint, hopeful smile crossed Clare's lips. Finally, she'd found someone who gave her credit for thinking about her plan. Unlike nearly everyone else, Dylan wasn't assuming that she was acting on mindless emotion.

"You're probably aware that there are people in town who are irritated with me over what I'm doing," Clare continued, her comment directed at the sheriff. "There are people at the police department and city hall who think me conducting my own investigation makes them look bad." She shrugged. "Maybe you're in that group. But I've got a two-week window to work on this full-time before

I go back to work and that's what I intend to do. I want to take advantage of the interest I've stirred up and talk to people before their memories fade and there's no longer the possibility they could help me."

"I can't say I know how you feel, because I haven't had the same experience," Finley said. "But I know what it's like to see an injustice and want to do something about it."

The sheriff glanced at Dylan and then back at Clare. "I'd like to be kept informed of any information you uncover that could help my investigation into the attack on you today."

"I'd like to be her point of contact with the sheriff's department," Dylan offered.

The sheriff studied him for a moment before nodding in agreement. "Clare's goals intersect with my goals, so I think it's reasonable to budget some of your patrol time to assist her with her investigation. Hopefully, that will prevent another attack."

Clare's shoulders dropped in relief. This was the law enforcement support she'd hoped for, even if it wasn't coming from the agency directly in charge of Jessica's case.

She turned to Dylan, and he gave her a slight nod of encouragement.

The smile she offered him in return felt faltering, but she made the effort.

Sheriff Finley stood and Clare realized she and Dylan were being dismissed. After exchanging goodbyes, they headed toward the exit.

Knowing that the assailant who'd tried to kill her today remained at large was chilling. Clare would be putting herself in danger by continuing her investigation and she knew it. But at least, for now, she didn't feel so alone.

* * *

"If you want to drive to a repair shop in town to have that car window replaced, I can follow you there," Dylan said to Clare. "You can drop your vehicle off and then I'll take you wherever you want to go." They were seated in his patrol car in the lot at Garnet Park. The scene had been cleared by city police.

"I'd just like to go to my dad's house and tell him what happened. With as few of the harrowing details as possible." She looked toward the park and the distinctive tree where the attack had started. "I'd rather not give him nightmares."

"I understand." Dylan scanned the area for at least the tenth time since they'd arrived a few minutes ago. He was worried for her. Whether or not the creep was connected to Jessica Barlow's murder Dylan had no way of knowing. But he *wanted* to know. He wanted to find the creep and see him locked up.

Dylan didn't have the resources to unravel Jessica Barlow's murder case, but he would do everything he could to keep Clare safe while she questioned anyone willing to talk to her about it. He would do that for any citizen, he told himself, trying to ignore the pull of attraction he felt when he saw the courageous determination in her aquamarine-colored eyes.

Clare gestured at her car. "My dad's a finish carpenter and he's always got clear plastic sheeting in his workshop that he uses to keep the area surrounding his projects clean. I'll just tape some of that over my broken window for now." She rubbed her chin. "I have this week and the next to go over everything I know about the murder and try to find new leads, new evidence. I don't want to waste a second of that time, including finding an auto body shop and dealing with getting an estimate. I'll wait till I need to go back to work."

Dylan nodded. "All right, I'll follow you to your dad's house."

He watched Clare exit the patrol car and get into her own vehicle. She sat for a moment, and he thought she might still be too distraught from the attack to drive. He was about to get out and offer to give her a ride and suggest they come back for her car later, when he saw her bow her head and her lips began to move. He hadn't seen her reach for her phone from the purse that had been returned to her or fiddle with a hands-free device, so it was possible she was praying. He hoped that was the case. Prayer helped him when he was anxious and uncertain.

Clare lifted her head, then backed her car out of the slot and drove out of the parking lot. Dylan kept a close eye on her and their surroundings as they headed for the town.

The forest thinned and scattered buildings began to appear after they'd driven a few miles. Clare slowed and made a right turn. She continued along the road and turned again onto a residential street with houses on large, tree-filled lots. A short distance down she pulled to the curb in front of a Craftsman-style home with a shop beside it. In front was a work trailer advertising Barlow Custom Carpentry.

Dylan parked behind Clare and got out of the patrol car.

"Looks like my dad is home," Clare said with a hint of nervousness in her voice. "I thought he might still be working on a jobsite."

"You want me to go in with you?" Dylan asked.

"No, thank you." She ran her hand through her hair. "I just want to pull myself together for a minute before I go in. My brother should be home. I don't want to freak him out."

Dylan wanted to tell her that after all she'd been through, she had a right to feel however she felt, but it wasn't his place to say that. It was funny how Clare was a familiar person to him because of their work connection, and yet the more time he spent around her the more he realized he didn't really know her at all. But he wanted to know her.

Not that knowing her better would lead to a relationship. Absolutely not. In fact, he was decidedly moving in the opposite direction from anything like that. His childhood friend Henry Walsh, who'd also enlisted in the military shortly after high school, had gone on to work as a private security contractor rather than returning to Cedar Lodge after his final military tour was complete. Henry's employer provided security and rescue services around the world, and after a couple of online interviews combined with Henry's recommendation, they'd recently offered Dylan a job.

Dylan *needed* that job. He loved Cedar Lodge and it was great having his family and good friends nearby, but over the last year or so his life had developed an uncomfortable edge to it. Boredom wasn't the right word, but it was something similar. Restlessness, maybe. For as long as he could remember, he'd always felt like he should be *doing* something. He'd played football and helped with the ranch while he was in high school. Then he'd served in the Marine Corps. After that he'd come home and begun working as a patrol officer at the sheriff's department, preferring action on the streets over a higher-ranking position that would have him spending too much time at a desk. His job at the sheriff's department had kept him feeling fulfilled for a while, but not anymore. After thinking about his options and discussing them with his family, he knew what he wanted to do next.

Staying in Cedar Lodge and starting a relationship was *not* it. He respected Clare and admittedly found himself drawn to her, but he could not let that get in the way of his plans. He would make a point of staying until the conclusion of her investigation, but after that it would be time to go.

Meeting up with Henry and the team overseas and diving into more intense challenges than he typically faced in Cedar Lodge was what he wanted to do. He was sure of that.

Dylan took a mental step back from Clare, along with an actual physical step. It didn't matter if he found her appealing, he wouldn't let things between them go any further. He cleared his throat and glanced at the pathway to the front door. "You should probably get inside. I'll make sure your jacket is returned as soon as Forensics is done processing it."

"Thanks."

He walked Clare toward the door.

"Will you stay here tonight?" he asked. "It would be best if you weren't alone."

She shrugged. "I don't know. Probably."

"Do you plan to work on your investigation tomorrow?" he asked as they ascended the steps to the porch.

She nodded. "I plan to talk with one of my stepmom's former coworkers."

"I hope you're careful." He'd check in with her in the morning and maybe he'd be able to go along on the interview.

"I learned a big lesson today, believe me. I'll keep my

eyes open," Clare said. They stopped at the door and she turned to him. "Thank you for everything you did for me today."

"Just doing my job." Though maybe he'd gone a little bit beyond that. Learning about all she'd been through and finding out that she was forced to conduct a murder investigation on her own stirred up a strongly sympathetic feeling within him.

But he couldn't let things between them go any further. Because he had plans to leave town, and those plans weren't going to change.

After she went inside and shut the door, Dylan headed back to his patrol car, offering up a brief payer for her safety. It appeared that Clare had kicked over a hornet's nest with her investigation. Being "careful" might not be enough to keep her alive.

"This brings back so many good memories," Clare said the next morning as she listened to the sound of power saws and hammering at a campground retreat center on the edge of town. She turned to Andrew Brooks, the operations manager for Freedom Path Counseling. An auburn-haired man in his midthirties, Andrew had worked closely with Jessica before her murder.

"My dad met my stepmom when he came here to volunteer for the repair work needed after an especially harsh winter," Clare continued. "It became a family tradition for us to come out every spring to help prepare the retreat for campers."

Beside them a collection of cabins encircled an Alpine-style A-framed community building with laundry and shower facilities as well as a kitchen and dining hall. Freedom Path was a company that worked closely alongside

churches in town by offering faith-based counseling and facilities for church group camping events through the warm
weather months.

At the moment Clare and Andrew stood beside a hobby
horse where Andrew had been sawing a cedar plank when
Clare walked up.

Andrew smiled at her. "Your stepmom liked to remind
me and the rest of the staff that she met your dad here
every year when we started prepping for camping season."
His smile faded. "Jessica lit up when she talked about her
family and her joy was contagious."

A lump rose in Clare's throat and she had to look away
for a moment. She'd avoided the camp since the murder because she was afraid of the feelings that might get
stirred up by a visit. But being here now, she was grateful for the reminder that Jessica had touched the lives of
others and that she had not been forgotten.

Last night had been tough. Telling her dad and brother
about what had happened had been painful and they were
obviously upset. Later, anxiety had needled her until she
was forced to pace around the house and try to burn some
of it off. Mental images of the attack forced their way into
her mind and she couldn't stop them. They'd come at her
relentlessly, even in her sleep.

Dylan had called her early this morning and the con-
fident sound of his voice had eased her fears. He'd told
her that the initial database search for the gunman had
come back inconclusive and that he'd looked at some mugshots the detectives had compiled, but the attacker wasn't
among them. He'd assured her that the sheriff's department would continue trying to identify the assailant, and
by the time the call ended, she'd felt a soft, fluttering
feeling in her stomach that had taken her by surprise.

She'd reminded herself that she was looking for a killer, not a romantic relationship. Her focus needed to remain squarely on finding justice for her late stepmother, and not on the very capable and admittedly handsome deputy.

Clare forced her attention back to the present and the man standing in front of her. "So, I imagine you've heard about what happened to me yesterday." It seemed likely since the basic facts of the attack had made the news.

Andrew shook his head. "I don't know. Tell me."

Clare gave him a summary.

Andrew's jaw dropped. "I'm so sorry you went through all that."

"I'm here because I'm trying to get the cops to revisit Jessica's murder case. So far, the attack on me isn't reason enough for them to do that. I checked on that this morning with the homicide detective assigned to her case. He said they still need newly discovered hard, cold facts to make my stepmom's case a priority. So here I am, trying to gather whatever information I can. Do you have any ideas on who might have wanted her dead? You worked together and spent a lot of time together. Any chance you've seen or heard or thought of anything in the last three years that gave you a theory?"

He shook his head. "No."

"Her neck scarf was found recently tangled in shrubbery near her downtown office. Maybe she just dropped it getting into her car…and wind or weather or whatever moved it down the street and that's the whole story. Or maybe she struggled with somebody and that's when the scarf was dropped. Maybe somebody forced her into her own car and then drove her out to the park to kill her."

Andrew was watching her closely, a frown forming on his face.

Now came the *really* hard part. Clare squared her shoulders. "I remember that there was a falling out between you and Jessica shortly before she was murdered. I never did know what that was about."

Andrew's eyes narrowed. "Do you think I murdered your stepmother?"

"I have no idea who killed her. Or why." Clare did her best to keep an even tone.

Andrew shook his head. "Did Jessica say we had a falling out? Because I don't remember it that way. We were putting together a budget and we had some disagreements over spending priorities. There's never enough money for all the needs and it gets frustrating. That's all it was."

He seemed sincere and she believed him. "Thanks. I didn't mean to insult you, but I needed to know."

Andrew nodded, a frown still on his face. "I have to get back to work."

He restarted his power saw and Clare walked away. The sounds of other power tools buzzed around her along with hammering and the voices of workers calling out to one another.

Maybe she could cross Andrew off of her mental suspect list. It sounded as if the disagreement between him and Jessica had been significant, but there was no indication it would have driven Andrew to murder.

She headed back to the parking lot, glad there were other cars and people around. It made her feel safer. Hopefully, the attacker wouldn't come after her if she kept to places where there were potential witnesses.

As she approached her car and reached for the door handle, she heard an odd, popping sound. Kind of like an aluminum can being crushed, but different. It took a few seconds for her to notice a bullet hole in her car that wasn't there before. Another bullet hole suddenly appeared, accompanied by the weird noise and she realized she was under fire.

Someone was *shooting* at her and using a gun with a silencer!

The work sounds around the camp continued as normal. No one had realized what was happening and that she was in danger.

Clare dropped to the ground, but staying there might not keep her protected for long. The shooter could be on the move. She looked around frantically, but couldn't spot the attacker. Which way should she run? If she headed for the cabins, would she make herself an easier target? And what if she put the workers in danger and her actions caused someone to get shot? There were high school kids helping out today as part of the school systems community service program. There was no way Clare would put their lives at risk.

Think!

The shooting had stopped for the moment. Now was the time to act.

She pushed off and raced for the cover of the nearby trees. If she could stay alive long enough to get out of range of the shooter, maybe she'd find a safe spot to hunker down and call for help.

Bullets kicked up the dirt at her feet as she ran. At the same time, her racing heart sank. Maybe she wouldn't be able to find a safe spot out of range of the shooter. Maybe she wouldn't ever be safe anywhere.

FOUR

"Cedar Lodge Dispatch to law enforcement in vicinity of Freedom Path Camp and Retreat Center: Respond to report of shots fired and ongoing pursuit of woman by shooter."

Clare! A chill ran up Dylan's spine as he keyed the mic in his patrol car. She'd told him she was going to the camp to speak with one of her late stepmother's coworkers. She had to be the woman in danger. "Dispatch, SD-615, show me en route to the camp. I'm approximately three minutes out."

"Copy, SD-615. Caller has taken shelter inside the admin building. Contact him there."

"Copy." Dylan hit the lights and sirens and made a sharp U-turn before jamming his foot down on the gas pedal and picking up speed on the curving stretch of the two-lane highway. He focused his thoughts on the camp's layout. It included a cluster of buildings surrounded by forest with a branch of the Meadowlark River running along the westernmost boundary. There was a boathouse over the water, plus some storage buildings for sports equipment. Plenty of places for a gunman to take Clare and hide. Assuming Clare was still alive.

He turned into the camp's driveway. "Dispatch, show SD-615 on scene."

"Copy."

He rolled down his window and listened, but didn't hear gunshots or screaming. He didn't see any people, either. Just abandoned carpentry tools on the ground.

Clare's car was in the parking lot.

People hovered near the large windows at the front of the admin building with anxious expressions on their faces. He exited the patrol car and hurried to the front door, where a man with reddish hair unlocked the door and let Dylan in.

"I'm Andrew," the man said. "I'm the one who called."

"Anybody hurt?" Dylan asked loudly, with his attention on the group of roughly twenty people, scanning their faces in hopes of seeing Clare among them.

"No," an older lady with her arms folded over her chest responded. "But we're all very worried about Clare Barlow."

Dylan swallowed thickly as his fear was confirmed.

"Do you need a description of her?" Andrew asked.

Dylan shook his head. "Just tell me what happened."

"Clare stopped by and we had a brief conversation." Andrew took a steadying breath. "We said our goodbyes and she walked away. A short time later I glanced in that direction—" he gestured to the north "—and between the cabins I saw her running in the forest. Then I saw a man chasing after her."

"What did the man look like?"

"I couldn't see his face. Average size, wearing a hoodie. He had a gun in his hand."

"You heard shots?"

"Yes. After I got everybody to stop working and head

over here so they'd be out of harm's way, I could hear them. They sounded muffled, like the guy was using a silencer."

"Anybody missing from your group?"

"No."

"Good. Keep everybody in here. More officers are on the way. If a stranger shows up, don't let them in. If anybody wants to go out and get into their car and go home, convince them it would be better to wait."

Dylan keyed his mic and gave Dispatch a summary of what he'd learned. "I'm going to start looking around," he added at the end. The nearest responding officer reported he was ten minutes out and Dylan didn't want to wait.

He stepped outside and heard the click of the door lock behind him. He headed toward the grassy lawn in the center of the camp and the section of forest where Andrew had last seen Clare.

Nervous energy charged the skin on the back of his neck as he stepped into the shadowy woods. So far he hadn't seen or heard any sign of the gunman, but that didn't mean the gunman didn't see *him*. He broke into a steady jog and soon spotted fresh bullet scars on the trunk of a pine tree.

He desperately wanted to find Clare and help her. *Please, Lord, don't let me be too late.*

The shadows beneath the tree canopy were both helpful and problematic for Clare as she ran for her life. They gave her cover from the gunman chasing her, but they also created slippery, icy spots where the last vestiges of winter's thick layer of snow hadn't yet completely melted.

In addition there were branches and tree limbs knocked to the ground in times of harsh weather during the winter, along with entire deadfall trees. Clare was forced to leap over the obstacles, which sometimes caused her to trip and stumble while desperately trying to put distance between herself and the shooter.

Crack!

The gunshot sounded muffled, but she definitely heard it.

Lord, help!

She'd been running downhill on the gently sloping ground in a zigzag pattern, hoping to find a spot to hide, but so far she hadn't managed to get out of her pursuer's sight long enough to do that.

She was starting to panic and for a few frantic moments she couldn't think beyond her next steps. Then she caught her toes beneath a partially buried tree branch and went sprawling and sliding in the mud. Gasping for breath, she sucked in a mouthful of yellowed old pine needles and immediately spit them out.

Shaking with fear and adrenaline, she looked around and spotted the rustic wooden benches and a simple stage placed in the middle of the woods, where campers could stage plays or sing-alongs. A few yards away from the stage was a shed that had been turned into a refreshments stand.

Clare could hide inside and finally have a moment to call for help. The back door wasn't kept locked since food wasn't stored in there. That would be a dangerous enticement to bears.

But what if the man chasing her saw her go in? He'd have her cornered and then what could she do? Nothing. It was a risk she had to take because she was otherwise out of options.

She scrambled to her feet and started running again. A

sudden wallop of discouragement threatened to drag her down. Maybe no one at the camp had heard the gunshots or realized she was in trouble. What if she was completely alone in this fight for her life?

Closing in on the shed, she slowed to take a look behind her. Still no sign of her pursuer. She hadn't heard footfalls or gunshots for a little while, either. She grabbed her phone—she'd learned her lesson yesterday and now kept it in her pocket—desperately hoping she'd have a connection when she tried to make her call.

Look again.

Before putting herself in the confined space where she would have no escape, she looked behind her one more time.

Crack!

Thick splinters from the shed's heavily weathered wood sheared off the corner of the small building and tore stinging lines across Clare's face. Fear jolted and sharpened her senses and she noted movement in the shadows barely ten yards away.

Instead of going inside the shed, she ducked behind it. Despite the frantic hammering of her heart that pulsed all the way up to her eardrums, she was able to hear a person's voice calling out. But it wasn't the nearby attacker. It was someone farther away.

She heard the voice again. *Dylan?*

Excitement and anguish battled within her as she imagined the quick-thinking lawman showing up once again just when she needed him most. She wanted to call out to him, but she didn't dare. Not with the criminal hovering close.

A second gunshot, this one tearing off more of the plank at the corner of the shed, sent her running again.

She fled in the direction she'd originally been heading, down the sloping terrain toward the Meadowlark River tributary and the boathouse.

She heard more gunshots behind her but she didn't dare slow down to look.

Please, Lord, let Dylan be safe.

Finally clear of the shadows and tripping hazards of the forest, she reached the relative safety of the boathouse. Empty metal racks lined the interior, where kayaks and paddleboards and oversize inner tubes were kept in the summer. She hit 911 on her phone. Nothing happened. She looked at the screen and realized she was in the midst of a dead space and connectivity was a wash. Her phone didn't show a single bar.

Her glance shifted to the water flowing in the tributary. Melted snow that had trickled down the surrounding mountaintops and would wind its way to Bear Lake. It would be cold. Cold enough for hypothermia, possibly. But the alternative was to stand here and get shot.

Again, she looked at her phone. When she realized she was hesitant to get into the tributary because she was worried about the device getting damaged, she shook her head and let it slide through her fingers to the wooden plank floor. In this part of the forest, the thing was useless to her, anyway.

She dropped feet first into the shockingly cold water. When she bobbed up for air, her teeth were already starting to chatter.

She swam toward the riverbank, hoping the trees that lined it would keep her out of sight of the gunman. Once she escaped immediate danger, she would swim back to the center of the tributary where the current would carry her the couple of miles to Bear Lake. At the lake she'd be able to clamber out onto the grassy shoreline, where sun exposure should warm her up.

She listened for the sound of Dylan's voice or gunfire or any indication of what was happening, but all she could hear was the sound of water rushing over the nearby rocks and forest debris that had fallen into the stream.

Crack!

A shower of pine needles fell on her from overhead, where a bullet struck a tree.

She heard Dylan's voice calling her name just before she felt a hard thump on her head and then everything was over.

Dylan followed what he hoped was Clare's trail, first to a shed where he noted the scars from recent gunshots and then toward the small pier that held the camp's boathouse.

The familiar voice of Kris Volker crackled over his radio, reporting the cop's arrival at the camp and asking Dylan for an update.

"Shooter still at large," Dylan stated into his collar mic. "I'm near the boathouse."

"Copy."

Moments ago his demand that the shooter drop his weapon had resulted in an exchange of gunfire. Dylan had taken shelter behind a large boulder until the shooting stopped. When it seemed safe to pop his head up and look around, the assailant had disappeared. The killer could still be hanging around, but Dylan had decided to keep his attention focused on finding Clare. He'd quickly picked up what appeared to be her trail. At that point he'd run the risk of calling out her name.

Now, when he stepped into the boathouse but saw no sign of Clare, his heart dropped. Then he spotted her phone. He'd seen the distinctive case when she'd checked the device a couple of times yesterday. Clare must have been here, but where was she now? Had she lost her phone in a struggle with the criminal? Had he shot her and thrown her body into the water?

Dylan hurried to the side of the boathouse to look in the briskly flowing tributary for any sign of Clare. He quickly spotted something downstream, close to the bank, that looked out of place. The object was at a bend in the stream, and it took him a moment to realize he was looking at a body. *Clare!*

He keyed his mic. "I see Clare. She's on the east bank of the Meadowlark River tributary."

Acknowledgment came through the radio as Dylan ran out of the boathouse and along the riverbank toward Clare. He whispered an urgent prayer as he slid down the sandy riverbank, making his way through twisted tree roots stretching out toward the water.

"Clare." He was knee-deep in the water now, and reached to move a tree limb resting across the side of her head. It was still partially attached to a tree and appeared to have split from the trunk and fallen as the result of a bullet strike. *Thank You, Lord*, Dylan breathed when he discovered that her face was out of the water and she was breathing. He keyed his mic to relay an update and request immediate medical aid.

Clare's eyes fluttered open while Dylan was talking. She startled and began struggling to sit up.

"Hey," Dylan said softly. "You're okay. Help's on the way."

"A tree branch hit me on the head." She winced in pain and then added, "I want to get out of the water." Her teeth chattered as she spoke. "I'm tired of being cold."

Dylan helped her to her feet. Her clothes were soaked and she was shivering uncontrollably as they climbed up the riverbank. When they reached dry grass, Dylan took off his jacket and placed it over her shoulders, then he wrapped his arms around her, holding her close. "I'll try to keep you warm until Cole gets here with a heated blanket."

"Thank you."

Familiar voices drew near and paramedic Cole Webb and an EMT approached through the forest. Dylan waved them over.

"Did you catch the shooter?" Clare asked Dylan as the medics drew near.

Dylan shook his head. "No." Disappointment in himself nearly had him choking on the word. He should have captured that creep. Frustrated with himself, he looked away for a moment. Coming up short on any task he set for himself was hard to accept and he knew he'd be replaying this whole event over in his mind tonight while he figured out what he should have done differently.

Clare squeezed his hand and he turned back to her, returning the gesture. "Any chance you saw this jerk's face and can confirm that he's the same guy that attacked you yesterday?" he asked. "I wasn't able to get a good look at him."

She drew a deep breath and then released it with a heavy sigh. Her trembling had subsided. "I assume it was the same guy, but I didn't get a clear look at his face, either."

"Clare! It's a little too early in the season to go swimming," Cole called out as the paramedic and his partner approached. The two of them set down their satchels. The EMT drew a disposable warming blanket from his bag and unfolded it as he neared Clare.

Cole stepped up to begin his assessment and it was only after the medic gave Dylan an odd look that the deputy realized he needed to let go of Clare and move away from her. He did so reluctantly and he was not in the mood to think about why he felt that way.

"Hi, Cole," Clare greeted the paramedic wearily.

Cole got to work and Dylan turned his gaze toward the newly arriving law enforcement officers now moving through the forest searching for the assailant. The gunman most likely would not be found. Not today, anyway. It had been brazen of him to come to the camp where there were so many potential witnesses. And smart to use a suppressor to quiet the sound of his gunshots. This assailant was somebody who was relentless and thought ahead. A very dangerous combination.

Hopefully, the detectives at the sheriff's department would have success in identifying the man, and at that point, Dylan could come up with a plan to apprehend him. Right now he had no idea where to look, but he would think of something. This case needed to be resolved quickly for all the obvious reasons—like the threat to Clare's life—but also because he'd again found himself caring about Clare more than he'd intended to. The undeniable personal relationship that was developing between them wasn't going to lead anywhere and it needed to end.

FIVE

"I feel better, already." Clare offered Dylan the strongest smile she could muster as they exited the hospital. The deputy could have dropped her off there and then left, but he'd stayed the whole time and Clare didn't know what to make of it.

He'd gone beyond just doing the bare minimum to help her and she appreciated it, but she was also concerned. Especially after he'd rescued her from the stream and held her close until the medics arrived. She'd liked that a little too much. But she had no room for distraction in her life right now. Finding clues that could lead to the apprehension of her stepmother's killer was her absolute top priority. This wasn't the time for Clare to think about herself and give in to the tug of romance.

And even if it were the right time, she would never let herself fall for a sheriff's deputy. She'd endured enough trauma having the cops show up at the door three years ago to let her know her stepmother had been murdered. She would not spend her future afraid for her husband's safety when he left for work every day, fearful that officers would show up on her doorstep telling her that her husband was gone forever.

"I think you should rest for a day or two after all you've

been through," Dylan said. "In the meantime I'll follow up with detectives at the sheriff's department and see what they've learned about the shooter. Maybe he's been identified by now."

Clare shook her head. "I'd love to relax for a few days but I can't. I've only got twelve days left on my leave of absence from work."

"You won't get much accomplished if you collapse in exhaustion."

She attempted another smile. "I'll be fine. I bounce back quickly."

They reached the edge of the parking lot and both of them surveyed the scene to confirm that it was safe to proceed to Dylan's patrol car. Chilly unease made Clare jittery and she impatiently tapped the toes of one foot. Inside the hospital she'd felt safe, but out here she was excruciatingly aware she was a target for a killer who could be watching her at this very moment.

An ER nurse had found someone from housekeeping to run Clare's wet clothes through a dryer while Clare wore a hospital gown. The doctor had confirmed that Clare wasn't seriously injured, and since her only complaint was a headache, treatment would be over-the-counter pain meds.

"Shall I take you to your dad's house?" Dylan offered once they were inside his patrol car. "Probably not a good idea for you to get your car from the camp and drive there yourself right now."

"Thanks, but I'd rather you take me to my apartment." Admittedly, she was scared to go there. But she was scared to go anywhere. Whoever was after her seemed to find her no matter where she went. "I live in a Victorian house that's been converted into four apartments," she added.

"There's a shared foyer with a security lock on the front door and I'm on the second floor, so it's relatively secure. Besides, if the attacker wanted to get to me at my dad's house, it wouldn't be any more difficult than getting into my apartment."

She knew without a doubt that her dad loved her and would do anything for her. She loved him, too, and, she didn't want to go back to his house and potentially put him and her teenage brother in danger. Something she might have already done by going to her dad's house last night, she now realized, assuming the attacker hadn't already known where he lived.

"Look, I don't want to force my dad and brother into a situation they didn't choose," she added, reaching up to tuck her hair behind her ears.

"You sure they want no part of your investigation?"

"Dad made it very clear from the beginning that he thought it was a bad idea."

"Did he tell you he didn't want you to come to him for help after you were attacked yesterday?"

"No," she said after a slight hesitation. After she'd told him what had happened, her dad had hugged her and then asked her to tell her brother about the harrowing event since Steve was likely to hear about it, anyway. Better to hear directly from Clare. "Dad told me I was welcome to stay at his house anytime I wanted for as long as I wanted."

"Did he ask you to stop what you're doing?"

"He didn't, actually." It wasn't until this moment that she realized how significant that was. Could his feelings on the investigation have changed? Was he willing to support it? Or was that wishful thinking?

Dylan still hadn't pulled his patrol car out of the hospital parking slot. "You got knocked unconscious today. You should probably be around somebody for the next twelve hours in case you experience secondary effects. Unless you've got someone to stay with you at your apartment, I think you should go to your dad's house."

"Fine," she said tightly. He made a good point and she didn't need one more reason to admire him. She sighed and glanced over at him, her gaze lingering on the warm brown color of his cheeks and the strong, angular edge of his jawline. She was attracted to him, despite her determination not to be, and she found that annoying. She was good at focusing her thoughts—it was part of what made her an effective emergency dispatcher. Normally, she could compartmentalize her emotions and stay on task, but with Dylan so close beside her, it was more of a challenge to do that than it should have been.

He drove out of the parking lot and Clare's stomach did a nervous flip as she thought about the attacker who was still out there. She turned her gaze to the side mirror to see if they were being followed, but didn't notice anything amiss. Then again, she was no expert at spotting a tail.

"Any chance you got an update on the guy who attacked me yesterday?"

"Unfortunately, no. There should be another round of mugshots to review soon."

Was the assailant from yesterday the same man as the shooter today? Extremely likely. And did that mean once he was identified, they'd know who Jessica's killer was? Right now she had no way of knowing.

"What about you?" Dylan asked a short time later. "What do you plan next to further your investigation?"

"I have some ideas. I just need to decide where to start."

"What does that mean, specifically?"

"I'm not a detective but I know murder investigators normally put together a timeline for the victim, focusing specifically on the final twenty-four or forty-eight hours. I don't have Jessica's calendars or day planners since the cops kept them as evidence, so I'm having to rely on memory."

"It had to be tough for you to repeatedly think about what happened to your stepmother while trying to get an idea on who the killer might be." Dylan shook his head. "If it were me, I'd have a hard time doing that."

"You're right, it was hard," she said softly. "I went to the camp to talk to Andrew this morning because I remembered he and Jessica had a spat around the time she was killed. According to him it was a mild work disagreement. I also remember that Jessica had a lunch appointment the day before the murder at Mimi's Bistro. I don't think I ever asked her who she was meeting there. I just remember wanting to make sure she brought home some of the bistro's orange chocolate chip cookies."

Tears began to slip from her eyes. Of course her stepmother had brought home a big pink boxful of treats for the whole family. But she'd also had a couple of Clare's favorite cookies packaged separately in a bag and handed it to her out of eyesight from Dad and Steve because it was something special just for Clare.

"You all right?" Dylan asked. "We can stop talking about this for a while if you want to."

"I'm okay." She swiped at the tears and cleared her throat. She nervously checked her side mirror again to see if anyone was following them. So far she hadn't noticed the same car lingering behind them and she hoped that meant no one was tracking them

"I plan to go to Mimi's Bistro tomorrow and try to find

someone who was employed there around the time of the murder. Hopefully, they'll be willing to talk with me. Jessica ate at the bistro often since it was near her work and some of the staff got to know her fairly well. Maybe I'll learn something useful."

Dylan slowed the patrol car as they neared her dad's house. "I'll go with you tomorrow. It will probably be in the morning, but let me confirm things with Sheriff Finley first."

"Thanks."

"I have something I want to talk to you about," he said before they got out of the car. "Just to clear the air."

Clare's gut tensed. "Okay, what is it?"

"I've heard there were rumors floating around after the murder that your dad might have been involved."

Annoyance dropped with a thud into the pit of Clare's stomach. She was aware of those ridiculous rumors. She hadn't ever wasted any time even considering them. Did Dylan actually believe they were true? Disgusted, she huffed out a breath. "Are the detectives at the sheriff's department bringing that up?"

"Your biological mother, Margot, left everybody behind and moved to Florida. Your dad remarried and later your stepmother is murdered. Two wives—both gone, albeit in different ways. Cops are curious by nature and don't like coincidences. Is there a thread through all of this that needs to be followed? Anger issues with women, maybe?"

Clare turned to face him, frustration heating her skin.

"I need to ask," Dylan said.

Clare sighed loudly. "While going through the horror of having his wife murdered, my dad also had to withstand being treated as a suspect by the police. That whole span of time was awful."

She pressed her lips together, fighting to get her emotions under control.

"But Dad understood that murderers are often known to their victim," she continued after she'd calmed down a little. "He was aware that spouses are sometimes guilty of the crime so he tried not to take the suspicion leveled at him personally."

"It's standard procedure to question the whereabouts and behavior of a spouse after a murder," Dylan interjected.

Clare nodded. "Dad wanted the killer caught, so he answered Detective Graham's questions and then handed over his clothes to be processed for potential evidence. Our vehicles were taken for a few days, too, to be combed for clues. The house was swept by a forensic team."

"Again, I have to say that's not especially unusual," Dylan commented, "though I understand it could feel like a personal insult."

Clare raised her chin defiantly. "Of course they found nothing to suggest he'd murdered her. Detective Graham flew to Miami to question my biological mom. She told the cops that my dad was a great guy but small-town Montana life wasn't for her. She'd been born in Cedar Lodge, but from the time she was a teen she'd wanted to move away. She told them she didn't leave out of fear for her safety or anything remotely like that."

"Good to know."

"Yeah, well, if a law enforcement agency continues to suspect someone and keeps rumors about them afloat, it's pretty much the same as condemning that person without a trial." Her voice shook with anger and hurt. "Suggesting my dad was the killer seemed to be the only theory Detective Graham ever had for the murder and when it didn't pan out he just let the investigation languish until it became a cold case. Apparently the detective wasn't capable of coming up with any other workable theory of what had happened."

Exhausted by her outburst, Clare prepared herself for an argument, or at least for a cynical cop comment.

Instead, Dylan looked her in the eyes for a moment with a searching gaze.

She held her breath, because she'd really begun to hope she wouldn't have to conduct her investigation on her own. But if the deputy decided to buy into the meritless idea that her dad was the killer, then the two of them were going to have to part ways.

Dylan finally nodded his head. "Okay, I believe you."

His gaze lingered and Clare felt much of her anger dissipate. The compassion in his eyes made it clear that he understood how she felt. Finally, a cop had listened to her frustration and acknowledged it.

"Thank you," she finally said.

He nodded in return.

They got out of the car and walked to the house. When they reached the porch the door opened and Clare's dad stood there, his eyes wide with concern. "Honey, are you all right?"

"I am." She gestured at Dylan to follow her inside, where her dad wrapped her in a tight hug and took his time before letting her go. Her teenage brother stepped up and gave her an awkward hug that didn't last nearly as long but still meant a lot to her.

"Dad, Steve, this is the deputy who's been helping me,

Dylan Ruiz. And Dylan, this is my dad, Gary, and my younger brother."

They exchanged a few polite words before Dylan said he needed to return to work.

Clare walked him back to the front door, where Dylan reminded her to stay out of sight as she opened it. From beside the window, where she would not be visible to anyone outside who might be watching, her gaze followed the deputy as he returned to his patrol car and drove away.

A ripple of unease passed through her as her thoughts drifted back to the attempts on her life yesterday and today.

Pushing for a reassessment of Jessica's cold case murder was already coming at a cost higher than she had imagined. Even worse, she had not only put herself in danger. Anyone around her at any time faced the risk of getting hurt, too.

The following morning Dylan tapped the notification on his phone while standing in the foyer of Clare's apartment building waiting for her to come downstairs. He'd spent much of last night thinking about all she'd been through and wondering how she was coping with the tumultuous emotions stirred up by their conversation.

Dylan had picked her up at her dad's house and brought her to her apartment an hour ago so she could change clothes before they went to work on her investigation. He'd already been upstairs to check that the apartment was secure before ushering her in.

Now he looked at the message Sergeant Reid had sent. Detectives think this is the perp in the security video footage. Can you confirm?

Dylan tapped the attachment and saw a mug shot of

the assailant from the cabin. *Finally.* Relief washed over him and he texted a response. Can confirm. Who is he?

Waiting for the reply, Dylan heard Clare's apartment door open and close, followed by the sound of a dead bolt being slotted into place. When Clare walked downstairs and approached, he held up the phone for her to see the image. "Looks like they found the shooter."

"That's him!"

Sergeant Reid's reply arrived and Dylan turned his phone around to tap it. Name is Kirk Madsen. Priors are petty theft, assault and brandishing a weapon. Nothing comparable to the recent attacks, no current charges pending, last known address is Tacoma, Washington. BOLO has been issued.

"Maybe they'll catch him quickly and this will all be over soon," Clare said as they headed outside.

They reached the patrol car and Dylan radioed in his current position and destination of Mimi's Bistro.

Beside him Clare fastened her seat belt. He glanced over and noted the large bruise on the edge of her forehead and some scratches and a few smaller bruises on her face.

"You sure you're up to this?" he asked. She turned to him and he nearly lifted his hand to brush the hair away from her eyes. Instead, he gripped the steering wheel tighter. He had life goals that did not involve a romantic relationship or remaining in Cedar Lodge, he reminded himself. Unease and boredom with the routine of life was an itch he was determined to scratch. He had a job offer that would take him back to a life filled with challenges and the adrenaline rush he craved on a regular basis. The intensity of this current case was an anomaly. Once it was over, things would go back to being too quiet for his taste. And getting wrapped up in some kind of gooey emotions

over an admittedly attractive woman was not high on his
list of life priorities. Maybe someday in the distant future,
when the time felt right, but not now.

"I'm feeling the effects of the last two days," Clare said.
"But I can keep going."

She was tough, he'd give her that.

"Okay." Dylan began driving toward the center of
town. "What else is on your list of places to visit besides
the bistro? Maybe we can knock out a couple of stops before I get back on patrol."

"I'll try not to take up too much of your time," Clare
said in a frosty tone.

What was up with that?

"Jessica had a rough life growing up," she continued.
"She was in trouble with the law until she came to faith
and turned her life around. I'd like to track down some
of her family and friends and talk to them. I just need
to find out who they are and if they're willing to meet
with me. I also think it would be a good idea to talk to
the people working at the business a short distance from
Jessica's workplace where her neck scarf was recently
found. A witness might have seen her struggling with
someone. Probably wouldn't hurt to also see if I can find
an employee at Freedom Path Counseling to talk to besides Andrew."

"You don't think the homicide detective and his team
interviewed all those people?" Dylan asked. "I would expect that they would have."

"I don't know. But I do know he never managed to
come up with any suspects other than my dad, and I'm not
convinced he even bothered to look any further."

They arrived at Mimi's Bistro and went inside. Scents
of coffee and maple syrup filled the air.

"Table or booth?" a young man asked, grabbing menus from the host station.

Dylan turned to Clare since this was her endeavor.

"Hi," she said brightly. "Is there anyone here who's been employed at the bistro for at least the last three years?"

The host, whose name tag read Will, blinked in confusion.

"I need to talk to someone who was here back then," Clare explained. "Just a few questions."

Will glanced toward the kitchen and then the tables and booths where servers were taking care of the scattering of customers.

"It's important," Clare pressed.

Will's gaze settled on the badge pinned to Dylan's chest. "Let me get the manager." He turned and disappeared in the direction of the kitchen. Shortly after, a woman in khakis and a crisp white blouse appeared from that same direction and offered Clare a friendly smile. "Hi, my name's Mona. How can I help you?"

"Any chance you worked here three years ago?" Clare asked.

Mona nodded. "I was a server back then."

Clare squared her shoulders. "My stepmother was murdered three years ago and the case remains unsolved. I know she had an appointment to meet someone here the day before it happened." Her voice began to choke with emotion and she cleared her throat. "I'm hoping someone remembers seeing her that day."

Mona's smile faded. "Jessica Barlow. I remember when that happened. I'm so sorry for your loss."

"Thank you."

"Come on back into my office."

They followed her to a small room with a window facing the parking lot. Mona sat behind her desk while Clare took a seat in a visitor's chair. Dylan opted to stand in the doorway where he could keep an eye on the hallway as well as the office.

"I knew Jessica," Mona said to Clare. "She worked nearby and she came in often. I enjoyed chatting with her."

"Mom liked to talk," Clare said with a shaky smile.

It occurred to Dylan that Clare probably routinely referred to Jessica by name when speaking with other people to avoid confusion. In her mind, it seemed, she thought of her stepmother as Mom.

"Do you remember anything from the last time she came here?" Clare continued. "Was she alone? Was she with somebody? Did she seem upset?"

Mona thought for a moment. "I remember that last visit because of the shock I felt the next day when I learned about what had happened. I can tell you Jessica came in alone, sat at a table, then a short time later Rita Carbone came in and sat with her."

"Rita Carbone?" Clare shook her head. "I don't know who that is."

"Her great-grandparents founded Family Mercantile."

Dylan realized then that the old department store would likely be their next stop. It was within walking distance, but riding in the patrol car would be the safer option.

"Did you hear what they talked about?" Clare asked. "I've worked in food service. You can't help overhearing things."

Mona shook her head. "I don't remember anything."

"Did you notice anything unusual?" Clare asked.

"No."

"What about their demeanor?" Dylan interjected. "Did either of them seem anxious or upset?"

"Jessica was her usual, friendly self. Rita seemed tense, though. She was another of my regulars back then. Still is."

"Anybody follow them in?" Dylan pressed. "Or follow them out? Or seem to be watching them while they were here?"

"Not that I noticed."

Clare frowned slightly. "Did you tell the police about seeing Rita with my stepmom?"

Mona's eyebrows lifted as an expression of realization widened her eyes. "I didn't think to contact them and tell them about it."

"Jessica had her meeting here noted on her planning calendar though it didn't mention the person she'd be meeting with. Did Detective Anthony Graham, the police homicide investigator assigned to the case, ever question you?"

Mona shook her head.

"Did he question anybody here as part of his investigation?"

"Not that I know of. I suppose he could have come in when I wasn't working. But wouldn't you think he'd try to find out who'd waited on her and then ask for me?"

Clare nodded and pressed her lips together. Dylan figured she was probably thinking the same thing he was thinking. That the detective had dropped the ball on that aspect of the investigation.

"Thank you for your time," Clare said as she got to her feet.

"Of course."

"Thanks," Dylan added, as he made way for Clare to step into the hallway and then followed her out.

"Detective Graham knew Jessica came here roughly twenty-four hours before her murder and he didn't bother to interview the staff," Clare fumed as they strode to the patrol car. "He just latched on to the idea of my dad being the killer and he didn't bother to pursue any other theories."

"It's surprising," Dylan said. "I don't know the detective personally, but I know he has a good reputation. He's been on the police force for a long time. Hard to believe he'd get away with being lazy or incompetent."

"I'm not so sure it is just laziness or incompetence," Clare muttered.

Dylan was busy watching their surroundings, but when they got into the car he turned to her. "What do you mean?"

"I've wondered more than once if maybe letting the investigation fall apart wasn't just due to laziness or incompetence. Maybe it was intentional. Maybe Graham was trying to help somebody cover up the murder. Or maybe he's got some personal connection to it."

Dylan stared out of the windshield for a moment before starting the engine. He wanted this case solved so that Clare would be safe, and that meant he needed to keep an open mind and follow the clues wherever they went. "I understand why you feel that way and it's a theory worth considering, but we'll need to tread carefully."

He turned to Clare. "I'll tell Sheriff Finley about what we've learned. Whether she follows up on it with Chief Ellis is up to her." He exhaled. "I'm not just concerned about the detective's reputation being unfairly diminished if we make accusations, I'm also worried about the danger it could add to your life."

"Someone's already trying to kill me," Clare said. "How much worse could it get?"

The assailant could be successful. That's how much worse it could get.

Dylan drove out of the parking lot and headed toward

Family Mercantile. Maybe they'd find some answers that would lead to the resolution of Jessica Barlow's murder case. And if that led to facts proving the detective had intentionally not done his job properly, Dylan would do everything he could to get that taken care of, as well.

SIX

"How are you holding up?" Dylan asked, bending slightly to look at Clare through her open car door while she was still seated inside. They were in the Family Mercantile parking lot and Dylan had gotten out of the car and walked over to the passenger side. "Do we need to take a break?"

"I'll be all right." She glanced down before returning his gaze. "I suspected that something was wrong with Jessica's murder investigation and that there was a reason why it stalled. I shouldn't be surprised that my instincts were right, but I am. And I don't know why it was stalled."

Dylan rested his hand on the side of the patrol car. "A murder investigation is always intense. Trying to get a lead on who killed your own stepmother is bound to have moments that are overwhelming. We can stop this investigation anytime you want if it's getting to be too much. I can take you back to your apartment or to your dad's house and then come back and interview Rita Carbone, myself."

"No, I don't want to quit." Helping to get the killer captured would be a huge accomplishment. Life-altering, for Clare. But seeing the criminal locked up was not the only outcome Clare hoped for. Jessica Barlow had impacted so many people's lives in a positive way as a counselor.

Clare wanted to do that, too. Being an emergency dispatcher had satisfied her craving to help people for a while, but for the last few months she'd begun to realize she wanted to do more. She wanted to be a counselor like her stepmom and serve the people of Cedar Lodge. But she would not be able to focus on that or any other aspect of her future—including having a family of her own one day—until she got the police back actively working on the case and ultimately incarcerating the killer.

She had to press on. If she wanted to build the future she envisioned, she couldn't suspend her investigation just because she got frustrated. She glanced at the handsome deputy, grateful to have him working beside her.

She took a deep breath and got out of the car.

The Family Mercantile parking lot was a rectangle of cracked and chipped asphalt. The bricks comprising the three-story building had also been damaged by multiple Montana winters. Maybe there wasn't money in their budget for upkeep. She saw cars in the lot, but business didn't appear especially brisk.

"I can't remember the last time I shopped here," Clare said as Dylan pulled open one of the double doors and ushered her past him. "Though I remember coming here with my dad and Steve when I was a kid." Observing the threadbare carpeting, she said, "It looked a lot nicer, then."

"Some of the older businesses are having trouble competing with online stores." Dylan gestured toward a young saleswoman standing behind a display counter filled with moderately priced watches and jewelry. "Want to start with one of those store employees and see if they can point us toward Rita Carbone?"

"Sure."

They approached the saleswoman, who appeared to

be in her early twenties like Clare, with thick sable hair woven into a loose braid that rested on the front of her shoulder. "Good morning," she said brightly when she spotted Clare and Dylan approaching her.

Clare did her best to smile in return. "Hi. Could you help us find Rita Carbone?"

"I'm Rita. How can I help you?"

Despite the weight of pessimism that had started to take root in Clare's mind, she felt a ribbon of hope unfurl in her chest. Maybe Rita knew something important about the murder. Maybe this was the moment Clare would finally begin to understand what had happened to her stepmother. She cleared her throat and said, "My name is Clare and I'm here to talk to you about my stepmother, Jessica Barlow."

Rita's smile melted and she nervously ran her fingers over her bracelet and then straightened it. "What did you want to talk about?"

"I imagine you know she was murdered three years ago."

"Of course. Terrible. It was a loss for the whole community."

"And I believe you met with her at Mimi's Bistro the day before she died."

"Who told you that?" Rita's eyes flashed with emotion. Whether it was fear or anger or something else, Clare couldn't tell. But it struck her as an odd response.

"Someone who was working the lunch shift and saw you two together."

Rita lifted one shoulder in a half shrug. "I met her there. Guess I'd forgotten how close it was to her...um, to what happened."

"Did you notice anything unusual about her that day?"

Clare asked. "Did she seem nervous or anxious about anything?"

"Not that I remember. It's been three years. We just met to have lunch and chat."

Another salesclerk wandered over to them. She had short black hair and appeared to be maybe ten years older than Rita. She lingered beside Rita and after a moment Rita turned to her. "We're talking about Jessica Barlow." She and the second clerk exchanged glances that appeared to convey something meaningful but Clare couldn't tell what that was: the understandable awkwardness of talking to someone about their family member who'd been murdered, or something else?

"I'm Jessica's stepdaughter, Clare." Introducing herself to the additional clerk was the first thing Clare thought of to keep the conversation going, since it seemed to have stalled. "This is Deputy Ruiz," she added.

Dylan nodded politely.

"I'm Rita's cousin, Libby Santos. I didn't know your stepmother, but I know Rita thought highly of her."

Rita turned her gaze to the window facing the street. Her eyes began watering and she wiped at tears that began rolling down her cheek.

"Why are you asking about this now?" Libby asked while her younger cousin wiped away another tear.

Having composed herself, Rita turned back to face Clare.

Clare hardly knew where to start. "The investigation's come to a standstill and I'm trying to get it going again." She decided to phrase the rest of what she had to say as diplomatically as possible. Appearing to disparage the local police could be off-putting and make Rita less likely to help. "It appears there might be some people the police investigators never spoke to who could actually be of some help. Did the police ever speak with you?"

"Why would the police want to talk to Rita?" Libby's shoulders stiffened.

"To ask the same question I did?" Clare suggested. "To see if my stepmom mentioned being worried about anything. To find out if there'd been somebody in the bistro watching Jessica or maybe someone outside who seemed menacing and focused on Jessica as she walked away after the meeting."

"It was just lunch together and that's all," Rita said, her demeanor changing from sympathetic to detached and bordering on affronted. "I don't know anything that can help you. I'm sorry."

"We need to get back to work," Libby said to her cousin.

"How did you come to know Jessica?" Dylan asked Rita before she could walk away.

"I met her at church." Despite her attempt at looking tough, another tear escaped. She reached up to dab at it before walking away with Libby alongside her.

"How do you read *that*?" Clare asked when they were outside the building. "Was it just me or did you sense some weird energy?"

They got into the patrol car and Dylan started up the engine. "It's hard to say." He gestured at his uniform. "Some people get nervous around cops. They think they're being accused when someone asks questions."

"Do you think Rita knows something important that she didn't tell us?"

"It's possible."

Clare blew out a puff of air in frustration and looked out her window. "I don't want to waste any of the time I have to pursue this investigation before I need to get back to my job. We're near Jessica's office, close to where her scarf was found. Let's go there and see if we can find anybody to talk to. Maybe someone saw something unusual around the time of the murder."

"Did you come here before, to look around after Jessica's scarf was found a few weeks ago?" Dylan asked. He drove across the parking lot and pulled up to a brick building with signage advertising a sound equipment and installation company.

"No, I didn't." Clare rubbed her hand across her forehead.

"Are you feeling unwell?" Spending the morning questioning people about the murder had to be taking a toll on her.

Clare dropped her hand and dismissed his question with a shake of her head.

"I'm ashamed to admit it, but until fairly recently I avoided thinking about the murder as much as possible," she added a moment later. "I didn't want to be reminded of it. Not that I could ever forget." She muttered the last few words. "I assumed the investigation was ongoing and it was just taking a while to find the killer."

Dylan glanced around. He wanted to protect Clare while also making sure she didn't overextend herself. "Do you want to wait here in the car while I go inside and see if there's anyone working who was around at the time of the murder?"

"No. I'm going with you."

As they opened their doors and got out, Dylan noticed a city police cruiser rolling down the street.

The officer behind the wheel, someone Dylan had seen around town but didn't know personally, had her arm hanging out the window. She looked toward Dylan and lifted her hand in a slight wave.

Dylan returned the gesture.

Clare saw the exchange and stopped to watch the cop as she continued driving down the road. "I know people are talking about me at the police department," she said. "They're talking about me throughout nearly all of emergency services and in city government, too. My co-workers have told me about it and I've overheard some of it myself. Some people think of me as the distraught 911 operator who believes she can find clues to a murder that actual police detectives weren't able to uncover."

The earnestness of her tone and the expression in her blue-green eyes drew Dylan in and tugged at his heart. Clare was putting herself in danger with her investigation, she had to realize that. And yet she was still determined to do what she could to see the killer of her late stepmother face justice. Her courage and selflessness were admirable.

Dylan hadn't found himself attracted to a woman in the way he was attracted to Clare in a long time. Maybe not ever. But that didn't mean he had to act on how he felt. His years in the military and tours in combat had taught him to shelve his emotions and get the mission accomplished. His mission now was to work diligently at his job until it was time to leave and start his new career. He'd be interested in having a family when he met the right woman at the right time. But not right now.

The police patrol car made a turn and disappeared from view. "If helping me has the potential to create bad blood between you as a county sheriff's deputy and the city police force, let me know," Clare said. "I don't want you to feel as if you have to help me."

"My willingness to help you isn't personal," Dylan

responded flatly, because he was determined for that to be the case. Whatever emotional connection he felt with Clare at times was just some momentary blip and nothing meaningful. He had a *working* relationship with her, not a personal one.

"It's my job to protect everybody in this town," he added, making sure his tone matched his determination, "not just you. Though I won't be protecting the people of Cedar Lodge too much longer. I've got a career move planned. I'm going into international private security work." It seemed important to say that last part out loud, so she'd know he planned to leave town.

"Got it." Clare drew back as if stung. "And don't flatter yourself. I'm sure a lot of women are attracted to you because of the whole cop thing but I'm not. I'm not interested in a man with a dangerous job. I've had enough trauma in my life."

Dylan realized he should have felt relieved by her comment about not being interested in cops, but instead, he felt irked by it.

He brushed off his irritation. This tension developing between them was preferable to a pull of attraction that neither of them wanted to act on.

"If Jessica's murder investigation wasn't conducted robustly, that needs to be addressed," Dylan continued, determined to direct their conversation back onto a professional, unemotional, track. "Meanwhile, we know for certain that someone wants *you* dead." He shifted his gaze to the street. "You're an easy target standing out here. Let's get inside."

They walked into the business and headed toward a guy tapping at a laptop. During a brief conversation he told them he'd spoken to the cops when the scarf was found.

There were only a couple of employees around when the murder happened three years ago, and none of them had seen anything noteworthy at that time.

"So much for that," Clare said as they walked toward the exit. "The Freedom Path Counseling offices are just down the street. I know the cops questioned some of the employees there when the murder happened, but I'd like to stop in there and talk to them, anyway." When they stepped outside Dylan spotted an unmarked police car in the parking lot.

The driver's-side door of the blue sedan opened and a tall man with a square jaw and bristly salt-and-pepper hair stepped out. "Clare, how are you?" Cedar Lodge Police Homicide Detective Anthony Graham, lead investigator on Jessica Barlow's murder case, turned to Dylan and offered a slight nod in greeting. "Deputy."

The cop who'd driven by a few minutes ago had likely given Graham a heads-up on Clare and Dylan's location. After the initial attack on Clare, Dylan's police officer friend Kris Volker had told him there were city cops, specifically those who were friends of Graham, who felt that Clare's investigation was an insult to them and they resented it.

"Good morning," Clare responded to Graham, her shoulders visibly tensing as the detective stepped toward her.

"I heard you were over here. Figured you were following up on my homicide case and I thought I'd stop by to see if you'd learned anything."

The detective wore sunglasses that kept his eyes hidden and he didn't take them off even though the three of them were standing in a shaded area. It was a subtle intimidation tactic and Dylan didn't appreciate it.

"I'm doing what I can to help with my stepmother's murder investigation, which has obviously reached a standstill," Clare said. Dylan didn't know if it was nerves or anger that made her voice shake slightly. "We weren't able to find anyone here with helpful information."

Graham nodded. "I was sorry to hear what happened to you yesterday at the camp and the day before over at Garnet Park. I guess now you realize how dangerous it is to play at being a crime investigator." He turned toward Dylan. "Looks like the sheriff's department volunteered a deputy to keep an eye on you. That was nice of them."

The tone was patronizing and Dylan recognized the detective was trying to get a rise out of him. He ignored the bait and kept his expression passive. After a moment of awkward silence, Graham frowned, seemingly disappointed at the lack of a response.

"Getting yourself hurt is not going to help Jessica's case," Graham said to Clare. "And drawing out some unhinged person who's targeting you for violence thanks to your online posts and interviews and demands at city council meetings will only make your stepmother's murder investigation that much more clouded."

"You can't know that," Clare said. "You can't know for certain why a criminal named Kirk Madsen is trying to kill me. And you don't know that I won't uncover some new information about Jessica's murder. And why wouldn't you want me to do that if I can?"

Ego. He's afraid you'll make him look bad. And possibly for other reasons they hadn't discovered yet.

"What makes you think I wouldn't appreciate getting some new clues or evidence?" Graham asked. "That's what it will take to make Jessica's case active again. The Cedar Lodge Police Department has to make decisions based on objective calculations, not emotion. We only have so many resources to spread across multiple investigations. Homicides with a reasonable probability of getting solved go to the head of the line. It's unfortunate, but it's a reality we have to face."

Clare held his gaze. "That's a perfect explanation of why you should be *thanking me* for what I'm doing."

The detective laughed softly and without warmth. "I've got to get going. Let me know if you learn anything. And watch your back." He turned to Dylan before walking away. "You realize if the sheriff's department supports her attempt at a murder investigation and she gets hurt or killed, it's on you."

And if she did it *without* Dylan's support and got hurt, that would be on him, as well. She was going to keep searching for answers—that was obvious after the two near-fatal attacks didn't stop her. Detective Graham's attempts to warn Dylan off or insult him wouldn't change his commitment to protect her.

The detective drove off as Dylan and Clare got into the patrol car. The Freedom Path Counseling offices were within walking distance, but for safety's sake they would drive.

Clare shook her head. "I don't understand why he's so annoyed with what I'm doing."

"A lot of detectives are territorial." Dylan made the turn into the counseling center parking lot. "In their mind, their case is *their* case."

Clare gestured at the door of the counseling center. "If we learn something helpful here I'll be happy to share the information with Graham and he can take credit for solving the case. I just want justice for my stepmother."

Clare reached to open her door and Dylan gestured at

her to wait a moment until he took a quick look around. He couldn't help reflecting on the detective's warning. Clare's investigation had put her in serious danger. Justice was important, and Dylan's career was centered around trying to help people obtain it. But was the pursuit of justice worth Clare's life? Ultimately, that was not his decision to make.

He completed his scan of the area. "All right, let's go inside."

Dylan positioned himself close by Clare's side as he accompanied her into the building where Jessica had been employed when she was killed. He hoped they'd be able to work their way quickly through Clare's list of people she wanted to talk to.

Then, perhaps, she'd end her investigation. At that point they could go their separate ways. Clare would be out of physical danger, and Dylan wouldn't have to keep trying to establish emotional boundaries between the two of them.

Boundaries that got blurred with frustrating regularity.

SEVEN

"That was disappointing," Clare said to Dylan as she unlocked the front door of her apartment. "I'd really hoped somebody at Freedom Path Counseling would have information that would help us solve Jessica's case."

"Three years is long enough for people to forget things, especially small details that hadn't appeared related to the murder at the time." Dylan handed Clare the bags of food they'd just bought at Dill Pickle Deli and gestured for her to step aside.

She watched him enter her apartment and do a walk through before waving her in. She should have already purchased a home security system, but she'd been tired and overwhelmed by other, immediate concerns.

"When we finish eating, you're going to grab your laptop and whatever paper notes you've collected and I'll take you to your dad's house, correct?"

Clare nodded as she set their soda cups on her small dining table. "I need to pack some clothes before we leave, but I'll make it quick."

Dylan had already let her know that he was expected to put in a few hours on patrol this afternoon and she didn't want to keep him from that. Especially since the extra help he'd offered her this morning wasn't anything *personal*.

She couldn't hold back a slight *huff*, even as she tried to let go of his earlier comment and not allow it to bug her.

But *he'd* offered to help with her investigation. It wasn't as if she'd begged him to stay by her side because she couldn't endure a minute without his company. She was not the clingy type, as he seemed to imply. Not by a long shot. Her biological mother had wanted to ditch small-town life and move to a big, exciting city from an early age. Her dad had fallen in love with her and convinced her to marry him and stay in Cedar Lodge. That arrangement had blown up in everybody's face.

Dylan's implication that Clare was trying to latch on to him was insulting for so many reasons. Beyond that, she knew it was the sort of behavior that never came to a good end.

She took a deep breath and blew it out, determined to let go of her irritation with Dylan. It drew her attention from the more important things like figuring out how to uncover new information about Jessica's murder.

They washed their hands and then sat down at the table where they put their sandwiches and sweet potato fries onto the plates Clare had gotten from the galley kitchen cupboard.

The top of Clare's shoulder suddenly stung and then she realized she'd absentmindedly reached up to scratch the spot where the bullet had peeled off a layer of skin. A thin bandage covered the wound and it didn't hurt much. But if the projectile had struck just a few inches closer to the midline of her body, the injury could have been fatal.

Thank You, Lord, for protecting me.

Unease rippled through her body at the memory of what had happened, and what could still happen. A profound sense of loss hollowed her heart as she found herself missing her stepmother. Jessica would have known what to say to help Clare focus on her faith and remember that she was a strong, capable woman. How heartbreaking that the one person Clare would have most wanted to lean on during this awful ordeal was the one who was gone.

Clare wiped away the dampness at the corners of her eyes and ate a little more of her sandwich before turning to Dylan. "What do you make of this Kirk Madsen creep who's targeted me?"

"My theory is that he likely killed your stepmother and now he's afraid you'll be the reason he gets captured and locked up for it."

"But when he approached me in the park he said something like, 'You're stirring up the cops to take a closer look at Jessica's murder and *we* don't want that.' Why would he say that? Who else could be involved, and why?"

"Could be he's a hired gun and the police haven't uncovered that fact yet. So he'd be referring to himself and his employer."

There were so many unanswered questions. Clare could end up spending the rest of her life trying to unravel the mystery of it all. Her gaze slid back to the handsome deputy. Maybe she wouldn't ever be able to find room in her life for romance, or a family of her own. Not that she would consider that with Dylan, even for a minute. He was a cop and that alone put him out of the running as a potential life partner.

"If Madsen's a contract killer and good at his job," Dylan pondered aloud, "then he wouldn't have a criminal record documenting his career as a hit man." Dylan finished eating the last bite of his sandwich. "A professional hit of your stepmother would explain why there were no witnesses and no useful physical evidence left behind. A guy nobody in town knows comes over from Tacoma, does the job and then leaves. That scenario fits the situation. In contrast, when a murder is personal and committed in a burst of emotion, the killer is typically too caught up in the moment to avoid leaving some kind of evidence behind."

"And if he came over from Tacoma, a city hundreds of miles away, and had no personal connection to her, that would make the facts even harder to uncover," Clare added, warming to the possibility. "While law enforcement is searching for Madsen and I'm going over my notes tonight, maybe I should look for clues on who would have the money and wherewithal to hire a killer."

"Hire a killer *twice*," Dylan said. "The first time to target Jessica and the second time to target *you*."

So much effort was being expended to keep the truth hidden. Someone had felt threatened enough by Jessica three years ago to kill her. And they were now afraid of Clare uncovering their identity. Who was that person?

She glanced at Dylan. Frustrating as he might be, it had been a comfort to have him with her today so she hadn't been forced to question people on her own. Even if the comfort he offered wasn't *personal*.

Yeah, the memory was still needling her.

It really wasn't that big of a deal for him to have said it. It wasn't as if he'd directly insulted her. She didn't know why the stupid comment bothered her so much. But it did.

After they finished eating Dylan stood to stretch his back and check his phone for messages while Clare zipped her laptop into a case in the living room. Then she headed for the bedroom to pack clothes for her stay at her dad's house.

Dylan had monitored his emergency radio during the meal and hadn't heard anything related to the apprehension of Kirk Madsen, though sensitive information was often relayed via cell phone. Perhaps Madsen was back in his home turf on the Washington coast. If he really was a hit man—still just conjecture—two failed murder attempts could get him called off the job. Or it could cause him to double down on his efforts. Dylan glanced in the direction where Clare was gathering her clothes, grateful that the attempts to kill her had failed.

He walked to the bedroom entrance and leaned against the doorframe. "How are you feeling?" Maybe he sounded like a broken record always asking her about that, but he'd learned that she was the sort of person who powered through whatever she thought needed to get done. He was the same way and he'd also learned that in the long run it was better to take a break and give yourself time to recover whenever you could.

Despite having interacted with Clare through work before, he hadn't known anything about her personally other than that she was good at her job as a dispatcher. Now he was admittedly intrigued by her and couldn't set aside the growing feeling of connection between them that he really didn't want. She was a coworker of sorts and, in his opinion, that was one reason to keep his distance. Reason number two for avoiding emotional entanglement was that she was the victim of a crime he'd been assigned to respond to.

How much of the attraction she felt for him was genuine emotional connection and how much was an understandably frightened woman looking for protection from a killer? And if he allowed anything personal to develop between them, would he be taking advantage of a woman in a vulnerable state? That was the last thing he wanted to do.

The whole topic was a knot of messy emotions and Dylan wasn't crazy about messes or emotions. He also wasn't used to it taking this much effort to keep his feelings under control.

"I've got a headache, but I'm all right." Clare answered his question after tossing some T-shirts into her suitcase. She turned to him and his heart thumped a little faster after he'd just reminded himself that she was off-limits. No matter what he told himself, the truth was that being around her made him feel more energized.

He shook his head. Ridiculous.

Then he noticed the dark circles under her eyes and the upswing of emotion he'd just experienced began to flatten. He shouldn't be thinking about how he felt when Clare was under so much pressure. He wanted to make her feel better. In an instant all of the reasons he'd told himself why he couldn't and shouldn't get involved with her started to blur. He cared that she was tired and sad and he wanted to do something about that. He wanted to catch the creep who'd caused her so much pain and make him face justice. He wanted to get her the answers she wanted so badly, and bring her some peace.

What he *really* wanted right now was to take her in his arms.

"Hopefully, I'll sleep better tonight," Clare said. "That should help with my headache. But before that, I'm going to spend the rest of the day looking over my notes and planning who I want to talk to while I have you with me tomorrow."

"What about your dad? Would it be worthwhile to

brainstorm ideas with him? Does he have any theories on Jessica's murder?"

The expression in her eyes shuttered. "Like I've mentioned, he hasn't been especially keen to look into it. More than once he's said, 'What's done is done.' That we should leave the investigation to the professionals and keep our noses out of it so he and Steve and I will be safe.'" She laughed slightly without humor. "I guess that dream of us all being safe is gone, now."

"Is it possible someone threatened your dad? Could that be the reason why he wants you and the rest of your family to stay out of it?"

Clare's eyes widened. "You mean like someone threatened me by leaving notes on my car a few days before the attack in the park?" She shook her head. "That never crossed my mind, but it should have. He hasn't mentioned anything like that happening."

Dylan straightened and backed out of the doorframe. "Might be worth asking him about that and also asking what he remembers about Rita Carbone. Maybe your stepmom mentioned her."

"I'll do that." Clare walked to her closet for more clothes and Dylan headed for the kitchen to grab his soda.

Crash!

The sound of breaking glass in the bedroom sent him running back in that direction. He arrived to see sharp, glittering fragments scattered across the floor. "What happened?"

The window facing the vacant lot next door was broken. Clare stood beside it, her back pressed to the wall, obviously trying to stay out of sight. She didn't answer Dylan, and instead remained frozen in place with her hand gripping the base of her throat and her gaze cast downward.

Dylan stepped around the bed to see what she was looking at and spotted a metallic cylinder on the wooden floor.

"Bomb!"

It was a homemade device fashioned with a section of pipe. It had been thrown through the window but hadn't exploded yet. There was no way to know its capacity for damage or when it would detonate. Dylan sprinted to Clare's side and grabbed her hand, his touch startling her from her stunned reaction.

They raced out of the bedroom. Dylan's mind sped through the limited options they had to quickly get to safety. The front door was too far away, plus taking time to unlatch the dead bolts could cause them to end up getting pelted by burning shrapnel.

"Here!" He turned into the bathroom, pulling Clare along with him. He shoved aside a shower curtain and gestured at the deep tub. Clare got in and pressed herself flat to the bottom. Dylan clambered in after her and shielded her body with his own just as a loud bang shook the walls of the apartment. The explosion was followed by sounds of splitting wood and the rattle of metallic debris raining down onto the floor.

Dylan caged Clare's head with his arms while doing his best not to inhale the chemical-laden smoke and pulverized debris billowing through the apartment. He waited a moment for things to settle before pushing himself to his knees and then pulled his shirt collar over his nose and mouth to act as a rudimentary filter before taking a breath. Through the fabric, he caught the smell of something burning. Once he stepped out of the tub he could see black smoke snaking out of the bedroom toward the living room. The breeze moving through the broken window sent tendrils swirling toward the bathroom.

Behind him, Clare had gotten out of the tub.

Dylan keyed his radio, calling in the explosion and fire and giving the dispatcher the address. He also requested police units in case the bomb thrower had hung around to witness his handiwork.

"There's a fire extinguisher in the kitchen," Clare said. She darted past Dylan to get it.

Dylan looked in the bedroom. The window was completely gone, as was a huge section of the wall. Nails littered the ground, and it chilled him to think what they would have done to Clare if the device had exploded while she was standing nearby. It was a close call. The assailant must have seen her through the window.

Fire had taken hold of the curtains and turned them into blackened scraps that dropped to the floor. Flames had also gotten a foothold in the bedcoverings and they were rapidly spreading to the wall adjacent to the bed and the shelving holding books that covered much of one wall.

"Stand back!" Clare called out, racing in with a residential-sized extinguisher that Dylan could already tell would not be enough to completely extinguish the fire. She pulled the pin and squeezed the trigger while directing the foam toward the flames on the floor where the fire maintained its most virulent strength. Dylan sprinted to the kitchen, threw open doors until he found a bucket under the sink, filled it with water and raced back to the fire.

Clare was still spraying the extinguisher, but the stream of flame retardant had weakened considerably and was almost used up. Dylan flung water on the flames that were crawling up the bookshelves, hoping to douse it, but the amount of water he had wasn't nearly enough.

"We need to get out of here and get your neighbors out, too." Dylan said.

"Check on the neighbors." Clare dropped the empty extinguisher and grabbed the bucket from Dylan. "If anybody's home, ask for their extinguisher. We don't have sprinklers, so the landlord put an extinguisher in every apartment." She was already running to the bathroom to refill the bucket. "Maybe we can keep the place from completely burning down before the fire engines arrive."

Dylan hesitated, wanting to get Clare away from harm's way as quickly as possible. But he also understood the drive to fight to protect your home. And Clare had proven she was a fighter.

He headed for the front door, opening it slowly while his hand hovered over his gun. If he were a criminal and setting up an ambush, he'd be waiting right there. But there was no one lurking on the other side of the door.

He dashed over to pound on the door of the other second-floor apartment and yelled, *"Fire!"* Without waiting for a response, he hurried downstairs, where one of the apartment doors was already open and an older man stood in front of it clutching a fire extinguisher.

"Is Clare okay?" the man asked.

"Yeah, but we need that." He gestured at the man to hand him the extinguisher.

"Check on your neighbor," Dylan indicated the other first-floor apartment before taking the extinguisher and running back up the stairs.

The dark smoke had thinned somewhat and Dylan was surprised to see how much Clare's determined efforts had accomplished. He pulled the pin on the new extinguisher and squeezed the nozzle, focusing the spray on the book-shelves and the flickers of flame on the wooden molding just above it.

Approaching sirens wailed in the distance.

The scope of the fire was noticeably reduced and much of the area that had been engulfed in flames was now smoldering. Dylan set the emptied extinguisher on the floor, then took the bucket from an obviously exhausted Clare and quickly refilled it before dumping water atop a smoking section of bedcovering that appeared to be in danger of reigniting.

"Something big has to be behind all of these attacks," Clare said in a shaky voice, her gaze on the broken window and the black, burn-scarred sections of the floor and the wall. "What could Jessica have stumbled into that not only got her killed, but also has her killer so spooked by my investigation that he's willing to risk coming out of hiding to stop me?" She ran a hand through her hair. "Did Kirk Madsen murder Jessica and now he's trying to keep that covered up, or is he trying to help the murderer—a completely different person—remain undiscovered?" She gestured at the fire damage throughout the bedroom. "And why launch all of these attacks and risk drawing attention to a murder case that had already been left languishing by the police department?"

Dylan shook his head. "Those are the exact same things I've been wondering about, and I don't have any answers. Not yet."

"This isn't going to stop me," Clare said grimly. Her chin was lifted and her spine was straight, but exhaustion and fear made her voice shaky. Dylan finally risked wrapping his arms around her.

Clare leaned into him and he held her with her head

resting on his chest just above his heart. He couldn't help noticing that keeping her safe and offering her whatever comfort and protection he could brought a peace to his own heart that he hadn't felt in a while. In this moment, the edgy, impatient and almost bored feeling that had dogged him for nearly a year was gone. In its place was a sense of rightness and peace.

The realization alarmed him. He had plans to leave town soon and pursue a new career. It was something he *needed* to do. He'd known that for months. For all Dylan knew, this peaceful feeling with Clare might not last. Beyond that, he'd promised himself he wouldn't risk inadvertently toying with her emotions and he intended to keep that commitment. Reluctantly, he released his embrace and stepped back from Clare, forcing himself to direct his attention toward what remained of the window and looking to see if there was anyone out there. It didn't appear there was.

Clare began coughing. Dylan's lungs burned from the smoke he'd inhaled. The interior of the apartment smelled like smoke and some kind of chemical accelerant. Through the window, he saw red and blue lights flickering between the buildings and trees a couple of blocks away. Emergency responders were almost there. He turned back to Clare, who was still coughing, "Let's go out on the front porch and get some fresh air."

With the building at her back and Dylan in front of her as a shield, Clare would be safe from a potential secondary attack. He would make sure of it. He looked around the partially charred room. Since her home was so significantly damaged, right around now would be a good time to bring up something that had been on his mind since the attack at the camp.

"You realize Madsen has probably figured out where you stay when you aren't here in your apartment?" Dylan asked after they exited the front door and were headed down the stairs. "Your dad's house might no longer be a safe place for you to stay."

Clare stopped suddenly on a step and Dylan had to reach out and hold her steady when he bumped into her. She turned to him, her eyes wide with fear. "You think my dad and Steve are in imminent danger?" She reached for her phone in her hip pocket.

"I don't have any reason to think they'd be targeted unless they were with you. Do you have a place where you can stay other than your dad's house? A relative or friend you could move in with?"

"And put *them* in danger, too?" She shook her head. "I won't do that. But I could check into a hotel or get a room at a bed-and-breakfast." She turned and continued down the stairs.

"That seems risky to me," Dylan said, following her. "Madsen could potentially come looking for you there and launch another attack."

"Then what do you suggest I do?" Clare asked as she reached the ground floor.

"I live in town," Dylan said, "but my parents have a small ranch north of the Meadowlark River. Anytime I'm not working, I'm out there helping them. Neither of my siblings live at the ranch anymore, so there are extra rooms. I think you should stay at the ranch until things settle down."

Clare lifted an eyebrow in response. "Don't you think your parents should have some say about who moves into their house?"

"They're okay with it."

Now both her eyebrows were raised. "You've already mentioned it to them?"

"Hear me out. It's well situated to see anyone approaching the house from a good distance away. Also, my dad's a retired marine, so he can handle any situation thrown at him. My parents took me in when I was a baby despite the threats made by my drug-addled biological father, who would repeatedly show up armed and ready for a fight for the first couple of years. I was obviously too young at the time to remember it, but I've heard stories. Both my parents have serious backbone."

"You're adopted?"

Dylan smiled. He couldn't help it. As a small child his parents told him that he was adopted and that it meant he was specially chosen by them. The happiness he'd felt at their explanation still lingered all these years later, whenever he thought about it. "I know what it's like to have family who are not blood-related but they're still your real and true family. So I think I might have an idea of how you feel about your stepmother and what happened to her."

Clare's eyes glistened and she wiped away the unshed tears. Whether they resulted from what he'd just said or they came from lingering smoke irritation, he didn't know.

They reached the front door of the apartment building and he pulled it open. The downstairs neighbor who'd given Dylan the fire extinguisher was standing on the porch with two cat carriers each holding a squalling feline. "You all right?" the older gentleman asked Clare, a concerned expression on his face.

She smiled and nodded at him. "Yes."

"I checked the other apartments," the neighbor added. "No one answered when I knocked and I don't see their cars parked out here anywhere, so I guess they aren't home."

A Cedar Lodge police car turned onto the street and Dylan heard the growling diesel engine of a fire truck just out of sight behind it.

Bang!

A bullet struck the flower basket hanging at the edge of the covered porch, sending plant shreds everywhere. Clare hit the ground and Dylan spun to help the slow-moving neighbor down and out of sight. Lying on the porch, the elder man wrapped an arm around each of his cat carriers and pulled them close. Dylan turned back to Clare and crouched in front of her to place himself between her and the shooter.

Bang!

The second shot, aimed lower, hit the porch railing and snapped off a chunk of wood before ricocheting and burying itself into the side of the building.

Dylan tapped his radio. *"Shots fired! Shots fired!"* He looked toward Clare and then her neighbor. "Either of you hit?"

"No," Clare said.

The neighbor responded with a breathy, "I'm okay."

Dylan drew his gun and got to his feet, looking toward the source of the gunshots.

He caught a glimpse of a man in a hoodie running away. Was it Madsen? Dylan couldn't tell. The shooter leapt into the passenger side of a gray SUV, his feet still visible for a few seconds as it sped away with the door hanging open and obviously someone else driving.

Dylan keyed his radio. "Shooter westbound on…"

"Aster Street," Clare supplied as she got to her feet and began to assist her neighbor.

"Westbound on Aster Street," Dylan continued, adding on a description of the vehicle and what he'd just witnessed.

Two patrol cars raced down the street in front of the apartment building, lights flashing and sirens screaming, and then made the turn in pursuit of the shooter's vehicle, which had already disappeared from sight.

The fire engine pulled to a stop and firefighters hopped out. They grabbed hoses and Dylan gave them quick directions on the location of the fire that was still smoldering and in danger of reigniting.

"So now we know there's more than one attacker involved," Clare said in a stunned voice. "The shooter, who may or may not have been Madsen, and the driver of the getaway car." She looked at the bullet lodged in the side of the building. "I suppose they must have tossed the device through the window and figured if the explosion didn't kill me they'd just shoot me when I ran out the front door."

"Explosive?" her neighbor interjected.

Clare gave him a slight nod.

The realization of what *could* have happened fell hard on Dylan's shoulders. No matter how many times he told himself that he couldn't predict and prepare for every possible outcome, he still felt like he should be able to.

"I'm so grateful you were here," Clare said quietly.

Dylan shook his head. "It was your own stubbornness that kept you alive, not me. If you hadn't been determined to fight the fire, we might have rushed out of the building with the shooter waiting for us and things would have ended much differently."

Communications traffic continued on Dylan's radio. It quickly became evident that the cops pursuing the shooter had lost him. Dylan glanced at Clare. It didn't seem like the right moment to press her on staying at the ranch, but he hoped she would choose to. She needed to take every safety precaution that she could while conducting her investigation.

With *two* perps now working together to kill her, it would become even more challenging to keep her alive.

EIGHT

The drive from Clare's apartment to the rolling hills west of Cedar Lodge in the aftermath of the fire was tense but fairly quiet save for the sound of Dylan's emergency radio.

Dylan made a few turns to be certain no one was tailing them and Clare kept a close watch on her side mirror for the same reason. Sergeant Reid had arrived at the apartment before Clare and Dylan left, offering his assurances that the sheriff's department would continue their vigorous search for Kirk Madsen and his accomplice. He'd also offered to remain on the scene until the landlord arrived to secure the damaged apartment so that Clare could leave.

Dylan slowed to make a left turn onto a not-too-wide wooden bridge that would take them over a tributary of the Meadowlark River. Clare released a sigh when they made it to the other side with no one following them. They drove a little farther, the patrol car rising and then dropping between the low, forested hills. Finally, he made another turn onto a narrow road. "The ranch is up ahead," he said.

Clare looked to the right. Between the trees of a section of thin forest, she spotted the outlines of a rambling ranch house and a barn. As they drew closer, she could see stables and an attached corral with a trio of horses enjoying the afternoon sun.

"Your family trains horses?" she asked as Dylan slowed for the turn onto a dirt drive.

"Boards them."

There was a closed gate in front of them and Dylan pulled out his phone. He tapped the screen a few times and the gate lifted.

"My parents also do a little farming and run a produce stand from spring into fall, when they sell pumpkins," he added.

When they were further along the drive, Clare could see a large greenhouse along with at least an acre filled with rows of young plants beside it.

"My dad's family homesteaded this place back in the day," Dylan said. "My parents moved onto the property when Dad's military career ended."

He sounded almost breezy in his commentary, but sitting this close beside him Clare could sense the tension in his body. He'd remained vigilant the entire drive, continually checking his mirrors as well as their surroundings. Despite being on his parents' property, he didn't seem to relax.

As they got closer to the single-story ranch house, the front door opened. A couple of big dogs ran out, barking with their tails wagging as they bounded up to the patrol car as Dylan parked.

"Tommy and Annie," Dylan said. "Tommy's the brown-and-white one. It's anybody's guess what breed he is. The black Lab is Annie. Both of them have sweet temperaments and they're friendly." He turned to Clare. "You like dogs?"

"I love dogs," she said enthusiastically, despite the sink-ing feeling of guilt overtaking her. This was someone's home and it was a beautiful, peaceful spot. It was wrong of her to potentially bring danger and trouble here.

"Maybe this was a bad idea," she said, not yet moving to get out of the patrol car.

In front of them, a man with military-cut salt-and-pepper hair and wearing a Western-style shirt, jeans and a big belt buckle had stepped out onto the porch. He offered up a friendly wave.

"My dad's not *that* scary-looking, is he?" Dylan joked.

Before Clare could reply, a tall woman with bobbed blond hair who, like the man, appeared to be in her sixties also stepped out of the house onto the porch. A gray cat followed her out and hopped up onto the porch railing before starting to take a bath. "That's my mom and Lulu the cat," Dylan said.

"Why would you invite me here?" Clare demanded, realizing—but not caring—that the flash of frustration probably wasn't rational. "This is a beautiful home and you know what kind of monsters are after me." She gestured at her smoke-scented clothes and then shook her head. "You know what the attackers are willing to do."

"I am aware of how dangerous the criminals are," Dylan said calmly. "But as a family we've faced dangerous situations before. There are times when *somebody* has to do something to help. When we're able to, we want to be that *somebody* who steps up." He opened his door and got out of the patrol car.

Clare shoved open her door and climbed out, too. She glanced back in the direction of the road. What if someone had followed them out here without being seen? What if the assassins directed their next attack here?

A cold, damp dog nose pressed against her lower arm

and snapped her out of her spiraling thoughts. She looked down to see Annie wagging her tail so hard that her whole hind end shook. The canine pressed down on her fore-paws and issued a couple of barks as if offering an invitation to play. Then she ran off to a pile of pine cones, grabbed one, and took off running with Tommy barking and chasing after her.

Thank You, Lord, Clare breathed softly. She'd desperately needed that small, joyful reminder that she and her problems were not the only thing in existence. The world was still turning. There was still good in it. These playful, joyful dogs were evidence of that. Letting her spirit become calloused would not do her—or anyone—any good. This family was offering her help and she needed to accept it graciously.

"Welcome to our home," Dylan's dad said as he walked up to her and extended his hand. "I'm Ruben Ruiz."

Clare shook his hand. He gestured at Dylan's mom as she walked up offering a friendly smile. "This is my wife, Sharon."

"Clare Barlow. Thank you for letting me stay at your home." Her voice caught in her throat and Clare was surprised to find herself on the verge of tears. She'd been doing her best to stay strong, but right now she was having a horrible time trying to keep herself together.

"We're happy to help," Sharon said warmly. "Dylan has told us a lot about you and we're sorry for what you've had to endure. Both the attacks and the loss of your step-mother."

"Thank you." The thought of Dylan having talked about her to his parents gave her a strange, fluttery feeling that was both thrilling and terrifying. Of course he would have spoken to them about her before extending the offer for her to come stay. Still, the idea was unsettling. It meant he thought about her when he wasn't on the job. She wondered how much he thought about her. Her thoughts turned to him way more than she wanted to admit.

If these were normal times and a normal situation, finding out that she was on his mind when they weren't together could be a good thing. Maybe something that could lead to a lasting relationship. But nothing about their time together right now was normal. And they had life goals that would take them in opposite directions. Her to a career in town as a counselor and him to some undetermined place outside of the country, where he'd be chasing after danger.

The most terrifying part was that she couldn't seem to turn off her growing feelings for him even though she knew one day soon he would be gone and she'd be left behind with an empty space in her heart that he'd formerly occupied. That was the last thing she needed.

"Let's get Clare inside the house where she can rest for a while," Sharon said before turning to face her directly. "Are you a coffee drinker?"

"I am," Clare said, grateful to be pulled away from her thoughts. Maybe a little caffeine would help invigorate her. It might also help her focus better as she went over her notes this evening and planned how she would continue her investigation tomorrow.

"Have you got any bags we need to bring in?" Sharon asked.

"I'll grab everything," Dylan said. "You guys go on inside."

Yep, after some coffee and a little bit of conversation, Clare would open her laptop and review the notes she'd made. The most genuine thank-you she could give the

Ruiz family would be to uncover information that would help with Jessica's murder case so she could leave their beautiful home before anything terrible happened. She hoped she'd be able to do that.

"So we're going to go talk to your stepmom's half sister?" Dylan asked the following afternoon after they'd gotten into his pickup truck and he started the engine.

Clare nodded. "Her name is Dolores." After poring over her notes Clare had decided to contact the only member of Jessica's family she'd ever met. "Jessica's family weren't too happy when she came to faith and chose sobriety. Apparently they presumed she was judging them whenever she interacted with them, which was absolutely not Jessica's style," Clare continued. "But the disconnect became a rift that was never repaired."

"Sorry to hear it."

"I texted Dolores earlier today. She told me she had no theory about who murdered Jessica. When I asked if I could meet with her anyway to talk to her in person, she said yes."

"All right. Where do we find her?"

"She owns an automotive upholstery business, Auto Interior Repair, on the east side of town."

Dylan tapped the name into his phone and the location popped up. "Got it."

The deputy had gone into work very early in the morning and was now off-duty. He'd arrived back at the ranch a short time ago and had barely had enough time to change out of his uniform before Clare approached him with her plan. She'd inwardly cringed while asking him to drive all the way back into town and across to the east side, but it was something she felt needed to be done. It wasn't as if she had a lot of options on how to proceed with her investigation. He was probably tired, but he hadn't mentioned it.

She'd thought about him most of the day when she wasn't going over her notes hoping to pick up some hint related to Jessica's murder that she hadn't noticed before. Much as she wanted to put Dylan out of mind while she focused on her efforts to form an investigative plan, her thoughts had drifted to him. He'd selflessly placed himself in harm's way to protect her on more than one occasion, which made her feel secure and strong whenever she was around him. She hadn't even realized how much she craved those feelings until he'd offered them when she needed them most.

Due to his career choices, Dylan's own life would continue to be in danger even if the current assailants launching the attacks were captured.

Whether he was a deputy sheriff in Cedar Lodge or working as a private contractor in hot spots around the globe didn't matter. Both paths were dangerous. Clare wouldn't be able to live with either one of them. Having the police show up at the front door to let the family know that her stepmother would never be coming home again was not the kind of situation Clare could ever face again. While she respected anyone married to a person who dealt with danger on a daily basis, she knew she couldn't do it.

And yet, despite knowing that, her resolve to appear more aloof than she felt got shakier by the moment as they sat together in the confined space of Dylan's truck. Even though they'd only been side by side for a couple of minutes, her heart was already beating faster and strands of nervous energy spiraled through her stomach in a way that was beyond her control and frankly not exactly unpleasant.

She turned to him, her gaze taking in the breadth of his broad shoulders and the black, raven-like color of his hair. Of course she wouldn't reach out and run her fingers across the strands of his bristly, short haircut. But she wanted to.

Dylan turned to her, a frown forming on his face. "What?"

He'd caught her staring at him. She should have expected that. He was a cop after all—his job required that he be observant.

They'd reached the end of the drive and he brought the truck to a stop at the gate before tapping his phone screen to open it. Once the way was clear, he took a lingering look in both directions before pulling out onto the paved road.

Then he glanced at Clare as if reminding her that he was still waiting for a response.

"I was expecting you to give me an update on the search for Kirk Madsen and his accomplice," Clare finally fibbed. There was no way she was going to admit she was admiring his hair.

"Law enforcement across the region is on the lookout for them," Dylan said. "So far there haven't been any sightings. Sergeant Reid has his team looking into Madsen's background for clues on his habits, personal connections, credit card transactions and phone usage. At this point he hasn't left a discernible trail. Which increases the possibility that he's a professional hit man. Most people leave a digital trail because they aren't planning to do something that might require them to go on the run later. We don't have any information on the accomplice. He hasn't been identified yet."

"That's disappointing." What if after putting herself

and others in danger with her investigation, they ended up with nothing? Or worse than nothing? They could end up with two violent criminals on the loose looking to kill Clare and anyone around her.

She took a deep breath and directed her thoughts toward her goals for the next few days before she had to go back to work. She focused on an odd piece of information she'd uncovered online last night after deciding to do a little research on Detective Anthony Graham. "Did you know that Detective Graham has a son who's been in serious trouble with the law?" she asked Dylan.

He sighed. "Cop families have challenges just like anybody else. But to answer your question, no, I can't say that I was aware of that. I work for a different law enforcement agency and, as I've mentioned before, I stay away from gossip."

"In this context it isn't gossip. It's information that could be related to Jessica's cold case. Specifically to the fact that it was weakly investigated and then quickly sidelined. The son's name is Scott and he was arrested for burglary, possession of stolen property and possession of illegal drugs. All this happened right around the time Jessica was killed."

"So you think Detective Graham was distracted and that's why his investigation seems shallow?"

"That's one theory," she said cautiously.

"You have another?"

Clare wasn't sure if she wanted to say aloud what she'd been thinking. But Dylan was sticking his neck out for her, so the least she could do was be completely honest with him. "Maybe Detective Graham's son was actually involved in the murder or somehow connected to it. Maybe that's why Detective Graham tried to make my dad look guilty and when that didn't work he let the case fall apart and go cold."

The thought of a corrupt cop was terrifying. Especially one who, due to his experience as a homicide investigator, would know how to cover up a murder.

"That's quite a suspicion," Dylan said. "What evidence do you have?"

"None."

"That's not an accusation that should be thrown around without proof, and for now I think we should focus on whatever other ideas you have," he said in a tone that bordered on defensive. "After we meet with Dolores, who else do you know from Jessica's past that we could talk to?"

"Nobody. I've tried to contact other family members and her old friends but they won't talk to me. I don't know if that's because they don't want to discuss the murder, or if it's a case of them still holding a grudge against Jessica even after she's gone. I'm hoping that after we speak with Dolores today, she might give them a nudge. Maybe one of them knows something about Jessica's past that got her killed. An old feud or bitter ex-boyfriend or something like that."

"What do you know about this half sister we're going to visit?" Now that they were approaching the edge of town and its intersecting streets, Dylan scanned the area around the truck and looked into the rearview mirror more frequently.

Clare likewise felt edgier, and became more aware of their surroundings. A chill settled on her skin, reminding her of the lurking fear that they could be attacked again anytime, anywhere.

"Is there a chance Dolores would have wanted to see Jessica harmed?" Dylan prodded after Clare didn't respond right away. "Was there an inheritance she could claim with your stepmother out of the way?"

Clare's jaw dropped slightly. She hadn't considered anything like that. But then, she'd had no reason to. "Jessica didn't come from money."

"That you know of."

Clare turned to him and he met her glance. "I don't want to believe a Cedar Lodge homicide detective would throw a case to keep his son out of prison," Dylan said, "but I will at least consider the possibility since you've mentioned it. In return, you might press yourself to consider some unsavory possibilities, too, if you want to figure out who killed her and why. Or, at the minimum, if you want to uncover any motives that might exist for keeping the investigation a cold case."

"You're right," Clare said quietly. If she really wanted answers then she had to uncover whatever truths came their way, even if they showed Jessica had been someone other than who Clare had thought her to be.

They reached the east side of town and Dylan made several turns that eventually brought them to Dolores's auto upholstery shop.

"Does she know we're coming right now?" Dylan asked as he parked the truck.

"Well, I didn't mention you. But I told her I'd be over within a half hour."

He pulled open the center console and picked up a gun he'd placed there before they left the ranch. "We don't know who might be waiting inside and this isn't the time to trust anybody," he said in response to the surprise that must have shown on Clare's face. He tucked the gun into the small of his back under his shirt.

Clare's stomach knotted with anxiety. She wanted to

believe he was being overly cautious, but given all that had happened over the last few days, maybe he wasn't.

The business had an office at one end of a building that was connected to a row of work bays with roll-up doors. Dylan pulled open the office door and stepped in ahead of Clare to look around before motioning her to follow him. A woman stood from a desk chair and strode to the counter with a friendly smile. "Hi, how can I help you?"

"She has an appointment with me" a voice called out. Clare turned toward a small, slender woman with streaks of gray in her dark hair, standing in the doorway of an interior office. "It's good to see you," Dolores added as Clare walked over to her with Dylan close behind. "I'm just sorry it's under such horrible circumstances. What you're going through must be terrifying."

"It's good to see you, too." The moment felt awkward since Clare had only met Dolores at Jessica's funeral and hadn't interacted with her since then. She considered approaching Jessica's older half sister for an embrace, but decided it might not be welcomed, so she finally just took a step back and introduced Dylan.

"A sheriff's deputy?" Dolores gave Dylan an appraising look before turning and gesturing toward her office. "Come on in. Like I said in the text, I don't know anything about Jessica's murder. If I did, I would have told the cops." She slid a glance at Dylan as he adjusted the position of a chair so that he had a view of the open door before the three of them were seated.

"So, how exactly do you think I can help you?" Dolores asked.

"If you don't have anything to tell me related to the murder, then maybe we could talk about the investigation that happened afterward. Did the cops interview you or anybody else in your family after Jessica's death?"

Dolores shook her head. "No one interviewed me. If they spoke with other relatives, I never heard about it."

"Do you think you could get anyone in your family to change their mind and talk with me?" Clare asked. "Even if they don't know anything about the actual murder, they might have some background information about Jessica that could help us figure out what happened."

Dolores responded with a noncommittal shrug.

There was a light knock on the open door, and a young man stood outside the office. "Sorry for the interruption." He turned to Dolores. "Johnson and Sons' delivery just got dropped off. Once again, it was short on some of the items we ordered." He stepped into the office and placed a packing slip on her desk.

Dolores sighed. "I'll give them a call and see what's going on."

The man nodded and walked away.

"My son, Joey," Dolores said with a slight smile directed at Clare. "He's not much older than you." She cleared her throat. "Last time I saw your little brother, Steve, he looked just like Jessica."

"Why do you think Jessica was murdered?" Dylan interjected.

Clare didn't miss the flash of irritation on Dolores's face before she tempered it with a more sympathetic expression. "I can only guess the reason for it. You hear of random killings by someone in the midst of a violent delusion or as part of a gang initiation. Sometimes somebody is in the wrong place at the wrong time and they see something that was meant to be a secret. Maybe it's for one of those reasons. I really have no way to know."

"She kept in touch with you," Clare said, her voice becoming shaky with emotion. Dolores was a living connection to Jessica, and sitting here now and talking to her brought a disconcerting wave of sorrow and loss that Clare had not been prepared for. "Did she talk to you about what was happening in her life? Did she mention anything she was worried about?"

"Don't have the impression that we talked often. We didn't. I know she was really getting into her *sobriety* support counseling," Dolores said with a quick eye roll. "Plenty of people can drink and it doesn't hurt them."

"True for some people, but not for others," Dylan commented.

Dolores turned to him. "Yeah, well, I didn't want to hear about it." She shifted her gaze back to Clare. "My conversations with your stepmother were brief. A little catch-up on who was doing what at the time and that was it. If you're asking for my opinion, I think you should follow up on some of the people she counseled. Maybe she annoyed one of them and they snapped."

Dolores leaned back in her chair and glanced at the packing slip on her desk. "If that's all you want to ask, I need to make a call and see why one of my main parts supplies keeps shorting my orders."

"Thank you for your time," Clare said as she and Dylan got to their feet.

"You're welcome." Dolores had already grabbed her phone. "Watch your back," she added. "I hope they catch whoever's been attacking you. And maybe the cops will finally figure out who killed my little sister, too."

Once they were back in his truck, Dylan asked, "So, what's your take on all that?"

"I don't know her well enough to read her. What about

you? Does your cop experience tell you she was lying or holding something back?"

Dylan thought for a moment. "If she's somehow connected to the murder, or knows something about it, or if there's a family secret she wants to keep hidden, she'd try to appear willing to help without giving away any useful information."

"Which is exactly what happened." Disappointment knotted in Clare's throat. "Were you surprised to hear that Detective Graham hadn't talked to Dolores?" she asked as Dylan returned his weapon to the truck's console.

"At this point, I can't say that I was. But as a routine step in an investigation, I would have expected Graham to talk to family members that live in town."

Clare turned to him. "Would you be willing to ask Kris Volker what he knows about Detective Graham and his son? Since Kris is on the Cedar Lodge police force, maybe he's heard something."

"I'll do that right now." Dylan pulled out his phone and tapped his screen. The call went to voice mail and he left Kris a message, asking him find out what he could about Scott Graham's legal problems and any impact that might have had on his father. After disconnecting, Dylan pulled the truck out into traffic and they headed back toward the center of town.

"I don't suppose there's any way we could look into Jessica's counseling clients and see if any of them seem to be a likely suspect," Clare mused aloud. She'd been thinking about Dolores's suggestion that the killer might be one of Jessica's clients

Dylan shook his head. "Privacy laws exist for very good reasons."

"You're right, of course."

As she considered her options, there was one name that popped into her mind, a person who was reluctant to talk but seemed like she might have some useful information. "Let's stop by Family Mercantile on the way back to the ranch and try to talk to Rita Carbone again," Clare said. "I can't help feeling like she knows something important, even if maybe she doesn't realize it."

"All right," Dylan said. "But we need to make it quick. It's getting late and it would be best to have you back at the ranch before sunset. Once it's dark, it'll be difficult to spot anyone following us. You can see headlights, but you can't see the vehicles well enough to know if any specific one stays behind you for a long time. Madsen and his accomplice probably wouldn't recognize my truck if they saw it, but I don't want to take the chance."

"Okay." Clare looked out at the lengthening afternoon shadows. She appreciated Dylan's concern, but the truth was she'd already been attacked multiple times in broad daylight. It was worth the effort to be cautious, but she really wasn't completely safe anywhere. Sadly, that was about the only thing she knew for certain right now.

NINE

Dylan didn't think Rita Carbone appeared happy to see Clare when they arrived at Family Mercantile. He thought she looked scared.

"Hello," Clare called out as she and Dylan walked up to Rita in the shoe section of the store. "Sorry to bother you again, but I was hoping we could talk."

Rita glanced around. There were a few shoppers in the store, but none of them were close by. She took a step back and leaned against a cart loaded with plastic-wrapped packages of sports socks that she'd been hanging on the nearby rack. "Hi." She turned to Dylan and gave him a polite nod of acknowledgment, which he returned.

Clare took a deep breath, her shoulders rising slightly as she appeared to organize her thoughts, then exhaled. "Rita, I'm not trying to put you in an awkward position when it comes to talking about Jessica's death. I don't blame you for the murder, I don't suspect that you committed it and I'm not trying to pin the crime on you. But after our previous visit, I can't help feeling like you know something about the killing that you're holding back."

"I'm not withholding anything," Rita responded with a pinched expression.

Dylan turned slightly so he would appear to be checking out the sneakers on the shelf beside him. He was in civilian clothes now, but he'd been in his uniform on their prior visit. Perhaps Rita was uncomfortable talking in the presence of a cop. He could avert his gaze in an attempt to take the pressure off her, but there was no way he'd step away and leave Clare unprotected.

"You must have thought about everything that happened to Jessica after we talked yesterday," Clare pressed. "And I know you met with her in the bistro the day before she was killed. What did you two talk about?"

"I don't remember what we talked about," Rita said in a brittle tone. "It was three years ago." She smoothed her blouse and appeared to collect herself. "I met her at a Bible study class. After that, she came into the store once in a while and we'd chat. Mimi's Bistro is close to her work and to the store, so we decided to meet there for lunch one day just for fun. That's it. We had lunch together the one time and then she was gone." Rita's eyes began to water and she grabbed a tissue from her pocket to wipe her nose.

"Is everything all right here?" Libby Santos, Rita's cousin and coworker, walked up with a serene expression on her face. "Something I can help you with?" she asked, taking in both Clare and Dylan.

"Everything's fine." Rita drew in a breath and shook her head. She dabbed at her eyes with the tissue and offered Clare and Dylan a trembling, apologetic smile. "I'm sorry. It's just that you're right, I have been thinking about Jessica since you came in yesterday and it's got me feeling sad and kind of touchy, I suppose." She lifted her chin, composed her expression and tucked her hair behind her ears. "Your stepmother was a wonderful person. Her passing was a terrible loss."

Dylan had done his fair share of questioning suspects

and witnesses, but determining if Rita was telling the truth was challenging. There were moments when her gestures and the tone of voice made it seem as if she was being secretive and duplicitous, but also moments where she seemed to be speaking the truth.

"You saw how upset I was when Jessica was killed," Rita said to her cousin standing beside her. "Thinking about it now is dredging up those emotions all over again." She shifted her attention to Clare. "I can't imagine how horrible all of this has been and still is for you. If there was anything I could do to help find the killer, I would do it."

"But you don't know anything about it," Libby said.

Rita shook her head.

Dylan glanced at Clare. She must have picked up the effort Libby put into directing the conversation. But Clare was still looking at Rita and not at him.

He shifted his attention toward the sound of approaching footsteps and turned to see a well-dressed man, possibly in his early fifties, walking up to them.

"Ah, here are my top sales associates," the man said smoothly.

There was no mistaking the gentleman. He was Max Durand, the family member who'd stepped up to take over Family Mercantile after the last of the old guard passed away. For a time there'd been conjecture that the store, a Cedar Lodge mainstay for over a century, would be sold off. But Max had bought out the interests of all the other family members and had retooled the business, doing lots of advertising that included his own face as the symbol of the updated shopping experience that people in town wanted.

Max's takeover had happened close to ten years ago, and from what Dylan could see, things had not gone well.

As with the last visit, there weren't a lot of shoppers in the store and the physical representation didn't look great. Possibly because there wasn't enough income to keep the store looking fresh and well stocked.

"There's a lady in the handbag section who looks as if she'd appreciate some assistance," Max said to Rita. "And you're always so good with that. Would you go help her?"

"Of course." Rita turned to Clare. "Please excuse me." She gave Dylan a polite nod before walking away.

"And you're in good hands here with Libby if you're looking for shoes," Max added with what struck Dylan as a little too much warmth in his voice for it to sound natural. The tone certainly didn't match the flinty expression in the storeowner's eyes. Was Max somehow aware of the topic of the conversation between Clare and Rita? Or was he just anxious to make the sales his store obviously needed and annoyed by his employees wasting time chatting instead of selling?

"Thank you, but I think we'll just browse around the store a little on our own," Clare said.

"Of course." Max smiled brightly. "Please do ask if you need any help."

Clare turned toward Dylan. She gave him a meaningful look that lingered as she walked closer to him.

"Rita never did answer your question regarding what she and Jessica talked about at the bistro," Dylan said quietly.

"I noticed that." They stepped from the carpeted area to a wooden floor walkway and headed toward the front entrance. "I can't figure out of Rita knows something related to the murder that she's afraid to tell us, or if she just talked to Jessica about something personal and she figures it's not my business, which I would completely understand. I just wish she'd make it clear if that's the case."

Without warning Clare veered off the walkway toward the section of the store with purses and wallets. Dylan stayed on her heels until she found Rita standing at a sales counter. A customer was walking away with a purchase and Rita's smile dropped as soon as she spotted Clare and Dylan.

Clare grabbed a wallet off a display table and dropped it on the counter in front of Rita, effectively forcing a reason for continued conversation. "I want to buy this."

Rita picked it up and scanned it.

"Look, if you told Jessica something personal while you spoke to her I'm not asking for you to reveal that to me," Clare said while her transaction was processed. "I just want to know if she seemed worried, if she mentioned anything that troubled her, or if maybe you saw something odd. Somebody following her or watching her or something that might have made her uneasy."

"I'm not going to talk about any of that here," Rita said after a quick glance over her shoulder.

"Right." Clare took a pen from her handbag, tore off the bottom of the receipt from her purchase and wrote down her name and number on it before sliding it across the counter toward Rita. "Call me. Text. Whatever works best for you. *Please*."

Clare grabbed her purchase and they headed for the exit. Dylan took a step ahead of her through the door for a quick look around before indicating to her that it was safe.

Outside, deep shadows were settling over the river valley town. Clouds had rolled in and a light rain fell. Dylan couldn't get a clear view very far down the street or into the entrances of the alleyways on the other side of the road. Nerves twisted in his gut, as they did anytime he felt like Clare was vulnerable. While her decision to risk danger brought him anxiety, he couldn't deny that if someone he loved was murdered and the killer had yet to be brought to justice, he wouldn't be able to let it go and focus only on his own safety, either.

He gently grasped Clare's upper arm as they walked, keeping her close to him until they reached his truck and she climbed inside. Then he walked around it, pulling his gun from his waistband and dropping it into the center console since he was in civilian clothes and wasn't wearing a holster. After that he slid behind the wheel.

"I only need Rita to give me one small piece of helpful information," Clare said as they pulled into traffic. "It doesn't necessarily have to be the solution to the murder, just something to get the ball rolling again on Jessica's case so it doesn't stay cold." She'd mentioned that sentiment in various way before, and it sounded to Dylan like she was trying to reassure herself that what she hoped to accomplish wasn't impossible.

Dylan did his best to keep an eye out for anyone who might be tailing them back to the ranch, but the dusky light and continued rainfall made it hard to do that while properly focusing on driving. He was glad to see that Clare remained vigilant, checking her side mirror at regular intervals.

They reached the edge of town and started moving at higher speed along the winding highway. Several miles later, Dylan slowed and made the turn that would take them onto the bridge.

"Someone turned behind us," Clare said nervously as his pickup tires hit the wooden planks and made a low, rumbling sound. "Looks like some kind of commercial truck."

Dylan's gaze darted to the rearview mirror. "I see it." The Ruiz ranch was not the only ranch in the rolling hills west of town and the vehicle behind them didn't necessarily contain the attackers. Nevertheless, adrenaline sent his heartbeat racing. With one hand on the steering wheel, he used the other to reach for the console so he could grab his gun.

"They're speeding up!" Clare cried out before he could get the compartment unlatched.

Bam!

Her shout was followed by a sudden, gut-wrenching impact into the rear of the pickup that forced them toward the side of the bridge.

The world spun out of control and Clare couldn't do a thing about it.

The impact sent Dylan's truck careening across the wet surface of the bridge until its front bumper collided with a railing post, and the second hit set it whirling in a different direction. Clare fought to take a breath as shock and terror froze her lungs.

Lord, help!

"Hang on!" Dylan called out, though his words were unnecessary. Clare had already gripped the door handle with one hand and the edge of dashboard with the other while Dylan rapidly spun the steering wheel, fighting to control the direction they were moving. Spring temperatures meant melting snowpack and the creek beneath the bridge was filled with frigid water moving at a brisk pace. Getting forced off the bridge could be an attack they didn't survive.

Bam!

Another collision triggered the airbags. For several terrifying moments Clare felt the pickup careening without being able to see ahead of her to know if they were about to drop over the edge and into the water.

"Clare!"

She heard the muffled sound of Dylan's voice and reached to slide her hand along the seat until she felt Dylan grab it and hold on tight.

The truck began to drop downward and Clare's stomach dropped with it, terror reaching all the way to her bones as she anticipated the fall into the cold water. But a moment later the front tires hit something solid and she realized they'd dropped from the bridge onto dirt. The airbags were deflating and she let go of Dylan's hand to punch the cloth out of the way so she could see what was happening.

They'd reached the end of the bridge and the truck was at an angle where the front end was positioned on the muddy creek bank and pointed at the swirling water down below. With the next collision they'd be knocked into the water, where, if they survived the impact and swam to the surface, they'd probably get shot.

Dylan grabbed his gun from the console along with an extra clip of ammo Clare hadn't realized was in there. "We've got to get out of this truck."

"Right." As she unfastened her seat belt, the pickup's interior was suddenly awash in bright light. In the dented side mirror she saw that one of the headlights of the vehicle behind them was out, presumably broken from the impact with Dylan's truck, but the remaining one was bright enough to give the assailant a clear view of their targets.

Bang!

The bullet pierced the back window and tore off the corner of Clare's headrest before exiting through the front windshield.

Bang! Bang! Bang!

Clare threw herself to the floorboard, smacking her head on the glove box along the way. "Dylan!"

When he didn't respond she shoved her hair out of her face and lifted her head to look for him.

He was lying across the truck seats, his head not far from her own. In the midst of the terror and chaos, he appeared remarkably calm. "Get ready to run."

Clare gestured toward the headlight shining through the back window. "They'll see us."

"We don't have any other choice. Run toward the trees."

"And then what?" The forest wasn't thick around here. Hiding from the attacker—or attackers—wouldn't be easy despite the rain and darkness. Especially if the assailant had a flashlight.

"This road is a boundary line for the Bowen Ranch property," Dylan said. "If we can make it to the main house, they'll assist us. If not, we'll hide in the first outbuilding we find, call 911 and wait for help. We can't take the time to call right now," he added as the assailant vehicle revved its engine as if building up for another assault. "We need to *go!*"

He reached over and opened the passenger-side door.

The next thing Clare knew he'd climbed over her and had hold of both her hands while pulling her out the door with him.

Bang!

Both of them were outside now and they stayed crouched low, using the truck as a barricade.

"Ready?" Dylan asked.

Before Clare could answer, they were already running. Rain splattered her face as they raced toward the nearest cluster of trees with the attacker's vehicle in pursuit. They reached the edge of the forest, where the assailant's truck was forced to stop, but its headlight still illuminated Clare and Dylan as they desperately sought a place to take cover.

Bang! Bang!

The second shot struck a branch, partially tearing it from the tree and sending it swinging into Clare's face. Startled, she stumbled and fell forward. Dylan dropped down beside her and then turned and fired several rounds in the direction of the truck until the headlight finally went out.

Clare pushed herself up to a sitting position and shook her head, determined not to let disorientation from the head smack and fall push her deeper into fear.

"Were you shot?" Dylan asked.

"Just hit by the tree branch, I think."

"Tell me if any of this hurts." Dylan reached out with his free hand and quickly patted her arms, shoulders and legs before moving around to check her back. "I don't see any blood or bullet holes in your clothes."

"I'm all right." Clare took a moment to close her eyes and focus her thoughts. When she opened them, the world appeared fairly steady.

"We can't stay here, we're too exposed," Dylan said. "Can you stand?"

"Yes." Determined to get up and move, Clare gritted her teeth and pushed to her feet. She took a step and weaved a little, but then regained her balance, and they started moving at a brisk pace again.

"We've got to get some help out here." With his gun in one hand, Dylan grabbed his phone from his pocket with the other and tapped the emergency call icon. "Shots fired," he said into the phone as soon as Dispatch answered. They drew close to a thick old pine tree and Dylan signaled to Clare that he wanted the both of them to stop and press their backs against it, presumably so no one could sneak up on them from behind. He relayed their situation and location before disconnecting. As a dispatcher herself, Clare knew the operator would have told him to stay on the line to give arriving officers updates. But she also knew that sometimes that wasn't possible.

"Now what?" she asked in a whisper in case the attackers were closing in on them on foot.

In the quiet that followed, she heard the voice of Kirk Madsen saying, "Do you see them?"

"No," a second, unfamiliar voice answered. Probably the accomplice from the apartment attack.

Dylan grabbed Clare's hand and they began running again in the direction where Dylan had said there would be a ranch house. Clare was gasping for air when they reached the edge of a fenced meadow and they stopped so she could catch her breath.

She heard the unfamiliar voice again. The assailant was not far away. "I can't see much of anything with this rain. How about you? Do you have eyes on them?"

"I've picked up their trail," Madsen said, his voice sounding tinny as if coming through a cell phone.

Clare's blood ran cold.

"They're almost to the house," Madsen added. "Head toward me and hurry it up. We need to take care of them before they get there."

Clare turned toward Dylan. "Did you—"

"I heard," Dylan interrupted. "The ranch house is still some distance away."

He changed direction slightly and they came across a barn. He pulled on the door and left it hanging open.

"We're going to hide in here?" Clare whispered.

"We're going to try and buy some time." He grabbed her hand, abruptly turned and they started running until they reached a small wooden storage shed. Dylan opened the door and Clare immediately caught the smells of motor oil, gasoline and cut grass. Dylan ushered her into the cramped space, where she tried to find a spot between a riding lawnmower, a gas-powered weed cutter, and a set of shelves holding items useful for groundskeeping.

"What are we doing?" she asked in a whisper, her lips close to Dylan's ear so the criminals wouldn't hear if they were nearby.

"Cops are almost here," Dylan whispered with a glance at his phone screen.

What if "almost" wasn't good enough? What if they arrived too late?

"Hopefully, the attackers will see the barn door I left open, go inside to search for us and then get caught by the cops."

Clare frowned. Considering what Madsen had gotten away with so far, she was afraid he wouldn't fall for Dylan's trap.

A flicker of light flashed through the gap between the planks of the storage shed. From a cell phone, maybe? Clare grasped Dylan's arm and stilled as goose bumps rippled across her skin. It looked as if the assailants had bypassed Dylan's trap and were headed straight for them.

"If something happens, get behind me," Dylan said with his lips pressed against Clare's ear.

She nodded and moved her hand from his arm to his back when he turned to face the door.

Heavy footsteps slapped against the mud in the direction of the barn. It sounded as if Dylan's setup of leaving the door hanging open had worked and drawn the gunmen in. Clare held her breath, her heart pounding in her ears.

Bang! Bang! Bang!

The sudden barrage of gunfire inside the barn made her jump.

"Are we finally done with them?" the voice Clare didn't recognize asked after the shooting stopped.

"We've got to go in and make sure," Madsen responded.

What would happen when they didn't find Clare and Dylan's bodies? They'd probably come to the shed to look for them.

Clare heard a dog let out a throaty howl and then bark excitedly in the distance. From the direction of the barn she heard cursing followed by heavy footsteps. The barking dog and her own pulse drumming in her ears made it hard to discern which way the footsteps were going. Were the shooters heading toward the shed?

Looking for a weapon, Clare turned to the shelving by her elbow and grabbed a metal bucket holding some nails. It was heavy. She could swing at the assailants if she had to.

The shed door jerked opened and a light shone inside. Clare could discern the outline of a man. She also thought she saw the tip of a gun. Her muscles tensed.

"Dylan Ruiz? Is that *you*?"

"Tom!"

He must be the neighbor rancher Dylan had mentioned.

The light tilted downward and in the backwash of illumination Clare made out the heavily lined face of a man with a thick mustache. He turned to Dylan and then back to Clare. "Are you two all right?"

"Yeah," Dylan said. He moved to look past Tom and into the darkness behind him. "We've got shooters after us."

Clare heard sirens.

Tom stepped back from the doorway and pulled a walkie-talkie from his jacket pocket. "It's Dylan Ruiz out here in the mower shed. Got a woman with him and they said there are gunmen on the property."

"Copy," a male voice replied.

"I'll update the police on what's happening," a female added.

A German shepherd bounded up to the shed door with a young man close behind him. "Dylan!" the young man called out, "we were getting ready for dinner when we heard gunshots. Thought it might only be somebody doing target practice, but I turned on the police scanner just in case. That's when we heard the radio traffic and knew something bad was going down."

"I imagine the criminals are gone by now," Tom said, "what with the barking dog and the police sirens and everything."

Clare set her bucket of nails back on the shelf and followed Dylan out of the shed.

"Why in the world were they after you?" the younger man asked Dylan.

"It's because of me," Clare said. The weight of responsibility for bringing danger to so many people hung heavy on her shoulders. "My stepmother was murdered and I'm trying to find some kind of lead to help the cops figure out who did it."

"So now the killer is after *you*?"

"Looks that way." She glanced toward the flashing lights of the approaching cop cars.

"But you're safe now." Dylan wrapped an arm around her shoulders and pulled her close, resting his chin on the top of her head. "Thank You, Lord," he said quietly.

"Amen," Clare said softly. After all they'd been through, it felt good to be held by him.

Hopefully, the arriving officers would be able to track down the gunmen before they made a clean escape. But based on the way things had been going since Madsen first approached her at Garnet Park, Clare didn't think that seemed likely.

TEN

"Go ahead to work, son, and don't worry about your mom and me or Clare," Dylan's dad said to him early the next morning as the two of them stood talking in the kitchen. "If those gunmen show up here, we can keep them at bay until backup arrives. Trust me."

Dylan had slept fitfully the night before. The police hadn't found the shooters, though they had recovered the stolen delivery truck used in the attack. So far no fingerprints had been recovered that could help identify Madsen's accomplice. Kris Volker had been one of the officers responding to the assault, and after the search for the gunmen was finally called off, Dylan had spoken with him. Kris had gotten Dylan's voice mail, but unfortunately he hadn't been able to learn anything useful about Detective Graham's son. Scott Graham had been seventeen when he was arrested around the time of Jessica's murder, so the details of the charges against him had been kept sealed.

For the moment Clare's investigation appeared to be at a standstill, which might be a good thing. In Dylan's opinion she could use some rest. And he needed to put in some time on patrol.

Dylan looked at his dad and smiled. "I appreciate all you and Mom are doing." Ruben Ruiz might have gray in his hair and some extra weight straining at the T-shirt above his USMC belt buckle, but there was still plenty of steel in his gaze. There was also a pistol riding in the holster at his hip. It was a relief for Dylan to know that he could get on with his other responsibilities at the sheriff's department assured that Clare and his parents would be all right.

"In the aftermath of what happened last night, I've been assigned this section of the county for patrol," Dylan said after a sip of coffee. "If I pick up radio traffic of anything happening around here, no matter how small, I'll get here as fast as I can."

"Just make sure you stay focused. In your line of work you can't afford to be distracted."

"Copy that." Dylan reached for the last bite of breakfast burrito on his plate, dabbing it in salsa before popping it into his mouth. Standing at the kitchen island with his dad while talking and eating was something they'd started when Dylan was a kid. If his mom was nearby, she'd shepherd them to the kitchen table to sit down and eat. Or at least she'd try to. Dylan downed the last of his coffee and then went to fill his commuter mug from the fresh pot that had just finished gurgling.

Ruben cleared his throat. "Clare seems very nice," he said while Dylan's back was turned. "Your mother and I are glad you brought her here and that we're able to help."

Dylan spun around, sloshing hot coffee onto his hand and the counter before setting the carafe back on the warmer. "Oh *no*," he said, shaking his head, his racing heart not only due to the coffee he'd already drunk. If they started talking about him having a relationship with Clare that would make it real. And he didn't want that. "Don't get any ideas. I know Clare through work, so I'm going the extra mile for a coworker. Before all this, I mostly only knew her through her voice on radio transmissions. After I came face-to-face with her in the middle of that horrific first attack and then learned about all she was going through, I had to help. But it's not anything personal. Or romantic." He turned back to finish pouring his coffee. "I just want to be clear about that."

Ruben made a *tsk*-ing sound.

Dylan could picture the disbelieving expression his dad was wearing. And Ruben Ruiz was his *real* dad. Didn't matter what a DNA test would say. Once again, he found himself empathizing with Clare. Some people thought a non-biological family connection would always be weaker than a biological one. In Dylan's opinion, they were wrong.

"You've shown quite a commitment to helping her," Ruben pressed.

"Yeah, well, it's a *short-term* commitment. Sergeant Reid's joint task force with Cedar Lodge PD is working hard on locating the attackers. As soon as they're captured and it's safe for Clare to go home, our time together will end." So what if Dylan thought about Clare all the time? What did it matter if every time he had reason to lightly touch her or wrap his arms around her in an embrace, he was aware of a feeling of tenderness that took him by surprise?

Admittedly, the sense of unfulfillment and dissatisfaction with his life that had plagued him for so many months had vanished in the last few days, but that was because he'd been busy. It couldn't be because of Clare. He had plans already set in motion and they didn't involve a romantic relationship.

"Whatever you say," Ruben muttered. "What about the investigation into Jessica Barlow's murder?"

"There's nothing I can do about that. You would think the attacks on Clare would be enough to move it out of cold case status, but so far that hasn't happened."

"So I suppose you're still on track to go work that international security job with Henry Walsh?"

"Of course. Why wouldn't I be?" He nearly winced at the defensiveness in his tone and worked to calm it down. "It's time I go back to the intense work I'm trained for." He'd withstood the discontent and unease that had plagued him long enough. Even if his temporary partnership with Clare *had* given him a taste of peace and contentment, it would end as soon as the case was concluded. She'd said she didn't want a relationship with a man who worked in law enforcement and that was something Dylan was not willing to give up. His service to others and willingness to go up against violent criminals to help protect the citizens of his town was a major part of who he was.

"Just know you don't have anything to prove." Ruben took a sip from his mug. "There's no reason you can't change your mind and start to enjoy life a little more."

Dylan looked down at his coffee. His dad knew him too well. Always had.

In his junior year of high school, Dylan had not only attended classes where he earned excellent grades, but he'd also played sports, worked the ranch and helped coach the little kids in the church sports program. By the end of the year he'd run himself ragged.

That was when his dad first talked to him about dialing things back and told him he didn't have anything to prove. Neither his parents nor his older brother or sister had ever made Dylan feel any less a member of the family because he was adopted.

When he was little, he'd associated being adopted with

being specially chosen. But later he'd somehow picked up the notion that he needed to prove to his parents that they'd made the right decision when they adopted him. Consciously, he knew it was a ridiculous idea and he had no idea where it came from. Something he'd seen in a movie or TV show? A snippet of overheard conversation that he'd misunderstood? Didn't matter, it was how he sometimes felt.

His dad had figured out what was happening and had done his best to put a stop to it. Still, there were times when that old compulsion overtook Dylan. Like now, when he realized he thought a family of his own was a reward he hadn't yet earned. Something he didn't deserve to have.

"Quit worrying about me," Dylan said to his dad in a teasing tone and with a clap on Ruben's shoulder. "I'm just working harder than usual because things have been unusually intense. Beyond that, nothing about my future plans has changed. And don't encourage Mom to believe my inviting Clare to stay here is some romantic gesture. It's me doing my job and trying to look after the town I grew up in and love. That's all."

"If you say so."

The sound of shuffling feet drew Dylan's attention to the passage from the living room where Clare appeared. Clad in sweatpants and a T-shirt, she had her hair tied in a loose bun on top of her head and her eyes were at half-mast. "I smelled coffee," she said with an embarrassed smile. "Thought I'd invite myself to the party."

A tender feeling Dylan didn't want to identify vibrated nervously in his chest. She looked adorable. And vulnerable. And he wanted to protect her.

"No need for an invitation around here," Ruben said

while Dylan tried to get his thoughts under control and form a reasonable sentence.

The older man grabbed a coffee mug from a hook beneath a counter and filled it with fresh brew. "You're always welcome to whatever you need around here."

"Thank you." She picked up the container of cream on the counter and poured some into her mug. Then she shifted her gaze from Ruben to Dylan. "Good morning," she said shyly.

"Good morning." Dylan's thoughts shifted to wondering what it would be like to be married to Clare and sip coffee with her every morning. He had to admit the mental image had appeal.

While he was thinking his gaze lingered on Clare, and her gaze stayed fixed on him as well. Her attention shifted from his face to the badge pinned to his chest and then to the gun resting in the holster on his hip. "It's hard to wrap my mind around the fact that the danger we faced last night, and even before that, is probably routine for you," she said in a voice still a little scratchy from sleep.

"Not routine. But I've trained for challenging situations and been through them before." The majority of the challenges he'd faced overseas were decidedly more intense than anything Dylan had come across in Cedar Lodge.

Clare shook her head, the tendrils of hair sliding free from her loose bun and dropping down to hug the sides of her face. "I could never be married to a man who risked his life every day," she murmured into her mug as she raised it to take another sip. "Having to deal with a criminal taking away my stepmother was almost too much to bear. I couldn't go through anything like that again."

"You've mentioned that." Dylan knew her words were reasonable enough, but for some reason they stung. He wondered if she'd overheard some of his conversation with his dad about the potential for Dylan and Clare to become romantically involved. "Don't worry, I'm not proposing," he said briskly. "I brought you here to keep you safe until the attackers are caught. This isn't a courtship."

Clare's eyes widened and she arched an eyebrow. "When I spoke of the possibility of marriage, I never said I imagined being married to *you*."

"I'm going to go outside and get some work done." Ruben made a quick exit from the kitchen.

Dylan's jaw tightened. It was annoying to think of Clare imagining the two of them becoming romantically linked. It was equally annoying to have her so emphatically state that she *wasn't* interested in a romantic future with him. "As I've mentioned before, I have career plans that wouldn't work well with being married," Dylan said, figuring the explanation might defuse the tension between the two of them.

Clare offered an elaborate shrug. "Why are you telling me? I don't care."

Okay, that was irritating, too. Dylan took a deep breath, loosened his jaw muscles and then picked up his commuter mug. "Glad to know we're on the same page. I need to put in a full shift today and catch up on a few things. Not sure what time I'll be back."

"I'll be going over my notes again, trying to figure out what to do next." Clare sighed and her expression softened. "I want to thank you for all you've done," she said. "I really do appreciate it. You helped keep me from getting killed last night." She offered him a shaky smile. "And who knows, maybe I'll end up leaving town, too, like you. If the cops can't find the attackers, I can't just move back into my apartment after it's repaired and go back to my old life. And I don't want to move in with my dad and brother and put them in danger. My biological mom lives in Florida. Maybe I'll end up moving there. I've attempted to build a relationship with her over the last couple of years, but that hasn't gone well. Maybe it's time to try again." She didn't appear happy about the prospect of that.

"Don't give up hope." Dylan wanted to wrap his arms around her, but he headed for the door instead. "Local law enforcement isn't ready to give up on capturing Madsen and his criminal partner and I know I personally am not interested in letting them get away, either."

He opened the door and walked out, frustrated that he could no longer deny his feelings for Clare. Not to himself, anyway. Her cared about her and wanted her to be safe and happy. But he also knew he wasn't the man to offer her that on a lifetime basis.

Dylan headed for the farm truck he'd use to get to the sheriff's station since his own vehicle wasn't drivable. He glanced over at his pickup where it would sit until he could get it towed to a repair shop. The dents and scrapes and bullet holes were a haunting reminder of the viciousness of the attackers who were determined to find Clare and kill her.

No matter how Dylan felt, or how much he wanted to shake off his feelings for her and get on with his new career, it was imperative that he remain Clare's bodyguard until Madsen and his partner were finally caught.

Clare stared at the list she'd written on a yellow legal tablet. She'd gone over her notes and news clippings yet again, hoping to see something new. She hadn't. So then she'd tried writing down her thoughts with pen and paper in the hope the change in process might produce a new perspective or insight. She'd been disappointed.

Early-afternoon sunlight slanted into the ranch office where she was seated. The large wooden desk had been pushed against the wall beneath a window facing the front of the house, and every now and then she caught a glimpse of Ruben as he went about his work with the dogs Tommy and Annie trotting happily behind him. Lulu the cat seemed to prefer sitting on the porch and supervising.

Clare dropped her pen to the desk and ran her fingers through her hair. Her frustration over not detecting a new lead for her investigation was combined with aggravation over her feelings for Dylan. She didn't want to be attracted to him, didn't want to fall for him, and yet it was probably too late for that. It wasn't just his apparent physical strength that appealed to her, but his depth of character and calm confidence, as well. She'd seen for herself over the last few days that he was a caring man with a good heart. There'd been even more evidence right in front of her since she'd moved to the ranch and seen the loving and respectful way he interacted with his parents.

She shook her head and huffed out a breath. This was not the time for Clare to fall in love or make any kind of commitment to a man. It might be a long time before she could do that, because getting justice for her stepmother was such a big part of her life. There was no room for her to nurture a romantic relationship.

Her cheeks heated as she thought about their conversation in the kitchen this morning. It was embarrassing that Dylan could tell she had stirrings of feelings for him. Her only consolation was that despite what he said, his behavior revealed that he had feelings for her, too. But apparently they weren't serious.

She shook off her thoughts of Dylan and directed them back to her list. But staring at the handful of items on the yellow legal pad wasn't going to get her anywhere. She'd already sent text messages to some of Jessica's family members and former friends, asking again to speak with them, but so far no one was interested. Apparently her conversation with Dolores hadn't changed anything. And Rita Carbone hadn't contacted her, either.

Discouraged and lonely despite the warm hospitality of the Ruiz family, Clare decided she needed to talk to her dad and picked up her phone to call him. Maybe if she heard his voice she would get a feeling of connection and normalcy back into her life, at least for a few minutes.

He dad answered with a tense, "Are you all right?" instead of his customary greeting.

Clare had sent him a brief message last night telling him a little about the attack, but mostly reassuring him that she was okay. She'd hoped that the brief update would keep him from worrying. It sounded as if that hadn't.

"I'm fine, Dad," she said. He didn't need to hear about her bruises and sore muscles after being battered in a crash and then chased through the woods. "How are you?"

"I pray for you all day long."

His heartfelt words sent Clare to the verge of tears.

She heard a clanking sound in the background on his end of the call as if someone had dropped a tool. She swallowed thickly before speaking, determined not to cry. "Are you at a jobsite?"

"Yeah, but don't worry about that. I can take time to talk."

"How's Steve?"

"Your brother's okay. Worried about his big sister. Thinking about his mom a lot and missing her."

A second wave of emotion had Clare on the edge of crying, again. "I'm sorry, Dad. I figured I could keep the effects of this investigation away from you guys." She cleared her throat. "I guess I didn't realize how it might affect Steve emotionally."

"Don't blame yourself, honey. It's not as if he would have otherwise forgotten about his mother and what happened to her." Gary sighed heavily. "Your brother has been talking to me a lot over the last few days about what happened to his mother. *Your* mother. Maybe I tried too hard to shelter him after the murder and that was a mistake. He told me he was online looking for information and came across some items you'd written on social media. He also listened to the true crime podcast interview you did. He's proud of you. We both are."

Clare closed her eyes and let the silent tears roll down her face. She loved her small family, and she missed them. She realized this might be a good time to once again try talking to her dad about what happened to Jessica. Maybe this time he wouldn't quickly change the subject.

There were at least two specific things she wanted to ask him about. One was Rita Carbone and the other, Detective Graham's troubled son, Scott.

"When will you be back home?" she asked.

"In an hour or so."

"I might come by the house later if you don't mind." She wanted to see him, not on a screen but in person. And if she were there with him it would be a little harder for him to avoid her questions. On a phone, he could simply disconnect. "Maybe you'd like to come out to the Ruiz ranch," she added, offering him an alternative in case he wanted one. After all, she was a lightning rod for danger these days.

"I'd love for you to come home," Gary said. "I want to see for myself that you're all right."

"Maybe we could talk a little about Jessica and everything that happened." Clare stumbled over the words, afraid the suggestion would make him change his mind.

"Do you think I know things I haven't told you?" he asked, his tone tinged with disbelief.

"No, Dad. But I can't help thinking you might know some detail that's important but you don't realize it."

"Why don't you plan to come over for dinner," he said. "I'll make chicken and dumplings."

Her favorite dinner since childhood.

"Actually, I was thinking about coming over while it's still afternoon. It's dangerous for me to be out after dark these days."

"So we'll have a very early dinner."

She would get through the meal and conversation quickly to minimize her dad's and brother's exposure to danger.

"Sounds like a plan. I'll message you later to confirm the time. Bye."

With a flutter of excited nerves in the pit of her stomach, Clare tapped her screen to phone Dylan and let him know of the plan. She looked forward to hearing the sound of his voice more than she should have. She was also still grappling with embarrassment over her behavior earlier this morning. She wished she'd remained cool and calm instead of sniping at him. So he wasn't interested in pursuing a romantic relationship with her. So what? He had life plans that would soon take him not only out of Cedar Lodge but also out of the country. And she planned to get a counseling degree and build a career in town. It wouldn't be wise for either of them to be led by feelings that were probably just temporary, anyway.

Tension gripped her stomach as the phone kept ringing on Dylan's end. *Probably letting it go to voice mail so he can avoid talking to me, since I was so snarky this morning.* But then he answered. "Hey, Clare, what's up?" He sounded friendly and even happy to hear from her.

"Is this a good time to call?" she asked.

"Sure. I'm just in the office finishing some reports."

"Are there any updates on Kirk Madsen or his accomplice?"

"Not that I'm aware of."

Suddenly self-conscious about how much she'd been asking of him, she hesitated to tell him about the plans she'd just made with her dad. But then again, if she didn't do everything she could to find at least a scrap of relevant information, including talking to her dad when he seemed to be in the right mood, then all the danger she and Dylan had put themselves through would be wasted. "I want to visit my dad tonight," she finally said. "It's the only thing I can think of to do next and it sounds as if he might be willing to have the discussion that he's put off for a long time."

"Can't you just talk to him over the phone or in a video chat? It would be a lot safer."

"It wouldn't be the same. He'll be more inclined to relax and open up if we meet in person."

"Okay, I'll drive you there. Maybe I can get a patrol car to follow us there and then back to the ranch to keep the trip safe."

"Thank you." She ended the call with a polite goodbye and no further conversation despite her desire to hear his voice for a little while longer. She appreciated Dylan. Very much. Adopting the more detached, professional tone he apparently wanted seemed like the best way to show her gratitude.

Some added emotional distance between them was the best thing, anyway. In the end, it would make things easier when they went their separate ways. Which would hopefully be after Clare discovered the information she needed, the attackers were captured and everyone was safe again. But there were no guarantees any of that would happen.

ELEVEN

Dylan took a sip of iced tea. Looking across the dining table, he noted the similarity between the gestures Clare and her dad used when they spoke. They looked physically different, with Gary's hair and eye color being dark brown while Clare was blond-haired with blue-green eyes. But the one-shouldered shrug Gary offered when he was uncertain about something and his slight head-tilt when he was thinking about an answer to a question were both movements Dylan had seen Clare make many times.

He glanced at Clare's fifteen-year-old brother, who was seated across from him. Steve was a polite kid who looked a lot like Clare. Right now the teenager had his gaze fixed on the serving of chicken and dumplings on the plate in front of him. After Gary took a few moments to say a blessing, Steve quickly dug in. Dylan did the same

"How's work been?" Clare asked her dad after they'd all taken a few bites of their dinner.

Gary swallowed his food, dabbed at his lips with a napkin and gave her a sad smile, "Honey, you and I have things to talk about and I want to get through them as quickly as possible so you can get back to the Ruiz ranch before dark. I've already prepared Steve for this conversation so let's just get started."

Clare squared her shoulders. She was silent for a moment, with her head bowed slightly, and Dylan had the impression she was offering a silent prayer before she spoke. "First of all, I want to know if anyone's ever contacted you and threatened to harm our family if you looked into the circumstances of Jessica's death."

Her dad met her gaze directly. "No. I stayed away from investigating on my own because I thought the possibility existed that it could lead to some sort of retaliation against us, and I didn't want to risk that."

"Okay." Clare nodded. "Do you think it's possible that one of Jessica's clients killed her? Did she mention anyone she was working with who scared her or put her on edge?"

Gary shook his head. "Your stepmom never mentioned anything like that, but then she wouldn't. She was a professional and she respected her clients' privacy."

"That sounds like her," Clare said with a faint smile. "Dylan and I went to see Dolores."

"Who's that?" Steve asked.

"Mom's older half sister," Clare explained before turning back to her dad. "The only theory Dolores had was that a client might have killed her. Beyond that, I hoped Dolores would prod one of Jessica's family members or an old friend to speak with me, but so far that hasn't happened."

Gary glanced at Steve. "When your mom decided to change her life, after she chose faith and sobriety, her family and most of her friends felt like that was somehow a condemnation of them. She didn't criticize or condemn them at all, but they cut ties with her, anyway."

"Dad, have you ever heard of someone named Rita Carbone?" Clare asked after they'd all been quietly eating for a few moments.

"Rita? Sure. She's about your age. Mom and I used to

talk to her in church sometimes. Now that I think of it, I haven't seen her in while." He set down his fork. "Don't tell me you think sweet little Rita killed your stepmother?"

"Right now I don't know. Were you aware she met with Mom for lunch the day before Mom was murdered?"

Gary offered one of his half shrugs. "I might have known that and forgotten. Why are you asking about her?"

"I thought she might know something, and both times when I tried to talk to her it seemed as if she was hiding something."

"Having been accused of murder myself, I can understand why she'd want to stay out of an investigation. It's my experience that the police keep you on their suspects list even if you've supplied every possible bit of evidence to prove your innocence." Gary picked up his fork and stirred the food on his plate.

"So you don't know anything about Rita that would help my investigation? There was no animosity between Rita and Jessica? Or something Jessica seemed worried about regarding Rita?"

Gary shook his head. "The only person I remember her being annoyed with was her coworker Andrew."

"He seemed to remember their disagreement as not being a big deal."

"Maybe not to him. But they had significantly differing opinions on whether Freedom Path funding should be spent on adding more counselors and expanding programs, which was what your mom wanted, or hiring a management team that could fundraise more aggressively, which was what he wanted. Jessica commented a few times that she thought the distribution of Freedom Path funds seemed kind of wonky."

"Did she mention anything specifically that she saw

or heard that made her question the spending?" Dylan asked, his attention piqued. *Follow the money* was standard advice in investigative work.

"Just that an awful lot of it seemed to disappear without it being apparent where it went. She thought too much of it might be getting poured into executive salaries and perks."

"I remember Mom saying that helping people was important," Steve said quietly.

Clare leaned over and wrapped an arm around her younger brother's shoulder. "I remember her saying that, too."

Dylan's heart ached for the teenager whose mood had turned somber during the course of the conversation. It was painful to imagine what it would have been like to lose his own mother in such a brutal way at the age of twelve, as had happened to Steve.

"Who else is on your list of people you want to talk about?" Gary asked.

"Did you or Mom have any interactions with Detective Anthony Graham before Jessica was killed?"

"I didn't. I can't imagine that Jessica did, either."

"Did she ever mention anybody named Scott or Scott Graham?"

"Not that I remember. Who is Scott Graham?"

"Detective Graham's son. He's had some trouble with the law."

"Can you think of any reason why Detective Graham centered his investigation on you," Dylan interjected, "even if it seems ridiculous?"

Gary shook his head. "No. I'm convinced he tried to pin the murder on me to make himself look good. I suppose he thought it made him look bad to have a murder on his hands and no leads."

Dylan caught Clare's eye. "Has Clare mentioned that we think there's a possibility Graham under-investigated the case on purpose?"

Gary stilled. "Why would he do that?"

"Graham's son, Scott, got into serious trouble around the time of Jessica's murder," Dylan continued. "Maybe the detective was distracted by his own personal family issues. Or maybe he was afraid that his son had been involved and he undermined the investigation to keep Scott from going to prison."

"I know Mom sometimes worked with juvenile referrals from the justice system," Clare added. "I just wonder if she and Scott crossed paths at some point."

"I wouldn't know about that." Gary placed his utensils and napkin on his plate and pushed it away. "Any chance you could put together an argument to charge Detective Graham with malfeasance if he didn't investigate the case as thoroughly as he should have?"

"There's not enough hard evidence for that at this point," Dylan said.

Gary nodded at Dylan, then cleared his throat and turned to Clare. "I know you've been working hard on this at huge risk to yourself. But based on what you've said tonight and what you've asked me, it doesn't look as if you've been able to collect enough information or evidence to get Jessica's case reopened." He took a deep breath. "You're putting yourself in extreme danger with no discernible payoff. Don't you think you've done all you can and it's time to wrap this up? Maybe if you stop asking questions, the killers who're after you will leave you alone."

Gary's voice gentled as he continued, "Jessica's passed on and she isn't coming back. Finding the criminal who killed her isn't going to change that. If I had to choose between finding out who killed Jessica and your safety, I would choose your safety. That's what I want most."

Dylan watched Clare work to swallow back tears as her eyes glistened. "I love you too, Dad," she finally said, speaking to the clear emotion behind his words. "I've got a few more days away from my job and I'm going to investigate as much as I can between now and then. After that, I'll let this go if I have to. But not before then."

"We should get going so we're back at the ranch before dark," Dylan said. He got to his feet and Clare and the others followed suit.

Gary offered his daughter a shaky smile. "I wish you could stay longer, but more than that I'd rather have you get back to the Ruiz family ranch where you'll be safe." He turned to Dylan. "Thank you for all your help."

"I'm happy to do what I can," Dylan responded while texting the duty sergeant with a request for a patrol car to escort him and Clare back to the ranch.

Clare walked around the table to embrace her dad and then hugged her brother. "Love you guys," she said with a smile.

A moment later Dylan's phone pinged and he looked down. "Nearby patrol car on its way." Clare headed for the front door and Dylan stopped her. "Let's take the kitchen door." Slipping out a side door seemed like the safest option.

Dylan walked out into the side yard and looked around before indicating to Clare that it was safe to follow him. Standing by ready to get into his truck once the patrol car escort arrived so they could quickly get moving seemed like the safest idea.

"There's got to be a way to get more information about

Detective Graham's son and what kind of trouble he was in," Clare said as they walked. "The detective had an exemplary track record and yet it seems as if he intentionally undermined the investigation into Jessica's murder."

They'd stepped clear of a section of fence beside the house and Dylan's gaze was drawn to an SUV parked down the street. It slowly pulled away from the curb and headed down the road in their direction.

"We need to take a closer look at Rita Carbone, too," Clare continued. "When we spoke to Rita she made it seem almost as if she barely knew Jessica. But Dad talks like the two of them really were friends."

As Clare spoke, Dylan's gaze was locked on the approaching SUV and his heart began beating faster. He watched the vehicle slowly speed up, which was a reasonable thing for the driver to do. But then it suddenly accelerated. Dylan's heart pounded as he quickly tried to gauge if this was an actual threat and he needed to hurry Clare back into the house.

Bang! Bang!

Bullets flew from the SUV's passenger-side window and Dylan threw himself atop Clare. He covered her head with his upper torso and grabbed his gun, but hesitated to shoot back. This was a residential neighborhood and kids were home from school.

"Clare!" Gary Barlow barked his daughter's name from the front door.

"Dad!"

Dylan felt Clare start to move and he tightened his grip on her arm. If she ran toward the front step she would be an easy target.

The attacker's SUV stopped on the street in front of the house and the engine idled.

"Grab your phone and call your dad," Dylan said. "Tell him to stay in the house and be ready for us to come in through the front door since it's closer than the side door. We can't stay out here much longer."

She did as he asked. "Have Steve use his phone to call the cops," she added.

Her phone was on speaker so Dylan could hear Gary say, "He's already on it."

The SUV began to creep forward. Dylan's ranch truck, which they were using as a barricade, could not protect them forever.

Dylan slid his grasp from Clare's arm down to her hand and he gave it a squeeze. "We've got to move, *now*!"

They ran up the driveway toward the front of the house.

In the next instant Dylan heard the roar of an engine as the driver of the SUV hit the gas and sent the vehicle up over the curb and across the lawn, chasing after them and tearing up chunks of dirt and grass while an occupant fired at them.

The house's front door, which had seemed close enough only moments ago, was now too far away. If they didn't change direction they'd be easy targets for the attackers to drive over them or shoot them, or attempt to do both.

Clare must have come to same conclusion, because she tightened her grip on Dylan's hand and pulled him toward a line of tall juniper bushes. When they reached the tall hedge, she shoved her way through a narrow gap and tugged Dylan along behind her. They needed to get to safety, fast.

Clare had no doubt the attackers would make their way through the hedge and keep pursuing them. But at least she and Dylan had bought themselves enough time to catch their breath and the police should be arriving any minute.

Please, Lord, let Dad and Steve be safe, she prayed at the sound of bullets fired by the assailants striking the front of the house and shattering windows.

Beside her Dylan looked around. "We need to take cover."

"In there," Clare gestured toward the workshop. "Dad keeps it unlocked during the day."

Bang! Bang!

Bullets flew through the hedge seconds before the nose of the SUV shot between the sturdy junipers. But then it abruptly stopped as the front got caught up on the broken branches. The vehicle swayed from side to side as the frustrated driver gunned the engine.

Gary's towable work trailer didn't offer the best protection, but it was closer than the workshop, so they quickly took shelter behind it. Dylan still had his gun in his hand, barrel pointed toward the ground, "I don't want to risk hurting civilians unless I absolutely have to."

Bang! Bang!

They were hunkered down by now, unable to see the assailants, and it took Clare a moment to realize the shots were fired from farther away than the hedge. She risked a peek around the work trailer and saw the attacker SUV had backed out of the spot where it had previously been stuck. It was gone.

Through the ragged hole in the hedge she could see the torn lawn at the front of the house and her dad standing there holding a gun. Clare could do nothing more than blink for the first few moments as her mind registered what she was witnessing. Her dad must have fired the shots that stopped the attack. She knew her dad had courage. She'd seen him display it by the way he forged ahead with life after Clare's biological mother abandoned them and left town. She'd seen it again when her dad managed to hold himself and his family together after Jessica's murder.

Yes, she knew her dad had backbone. She'd just never expected to see mild-mannered Gary Barlow demonstrate it like this.

The sound of approaching sirens snapped her out of her stupor. Their police escort must have gotten word of the attack and it sounded as if a second cruiser had been dispatched to their home, as well.

"Dad!" Clare raced toward him.

"You're all right," Gary said wearily as he tucked away the gun at the small of his back and wrapped his arms around his daughter.

"I heard bullets breaking through the front window of the house while the attackers were shooting," Clare said, lacking the strength to hold back the sob that rose up in her throat. She began to cry. "I was so worried."

"Steve and I are both fine," her dad said, patting her back like he had when she was little.

On the street, red and blue lights flashed from arriving cop cars and Dylan hurried over to talk to the officers.

"I didn't realize you had a gun," Clare said to her dad.

"I bought it after your stepmother was killed. Just in case. Hoped I'd never have to use it."

"I'm sorry for stirring everything up." Clare worked to compose herself. "It just seemed wrong for someone to get away with murdering Jessica and I felt like I had to do something about it."

"Don't blame yourself. You're doing what I wanted to do but didn't dare because I was worried about our safety."

They began walking toward the cops. Steve stood on

the lawn and offered his sister and father a weary greeting as they approached.

The cops got back into their cars and sped off.

"I gave them a description of the SUV and they're going to see if they can find the attackers," Dylan called out to Clare. The deputy turned to her dad. "You and Steve should come stay at my family's ranch until things settle down. We'd love to have you there."

Gary shook his head. "Thanks, but I want to get Steve completely out of town. We've got family in Idaho. We'll head over there for a while." He turned to Clare. "You could come with us."

Clare shook her head. Despite everything, she wouldn't stop her investigation until her two-week leave of absence ran out. At that point, if things were still unresolved, she would have to give up and accept the situation. But she wasn't at that point, yet. "You guys go over to Idaho and do your best to stay safe."

She turned to Dylan and he wrapped an arm around her shoulder, pulling her against him and placing a kiss on her forehead. His warmth and caring helped her hold herself together when she was on the verge of hopelessness and tears.

Clare would keep going with her investigation as long as she had Deputy Dylan Ruiz by her side. How she would cope with missing him after he left town was something she would have to figure out in the future.

Hopefully, the two of them would be able to stay alive so they could have a future. But there was no guarantee of that.

TWELVE

"Don't give Dad any trouble, okay?" Clare smiled at the video image of her brother on her computer screen.

"What are you talking about?" Steve teased in return. "You're the troublemaker, not me."

It was early afternoon the day following the attacks at her dad's house. Clare had already spent several minutes on the video call speaking with her father before talking to her brother. The two of them were comfortably situated at a relative's house on a ranch in Idaho and Clare was grateful they were safe.

After the video call ended, Clare returned to reviewing the report she'd been working on, summarizing everything she knew, thought or suspected regarding the murder of Jessica Barlow. Unfortunately, it wasn't much. But she wanted to have something to hand over to the authorities after she wound down her investigation and returned to work. So far, it didn't look as if she'd be successful getting the cold case reactivated, and that was a hard reality to swallow.

Clare had included her questions about Detective Graham's competence and diligence in the investigation, because in the end, why not? Dylan had passed along word about what they'd discovered regarding the lackluster pursuit of the case to Chief Ellis and so far they'd gotten no response. If including it in her report angered the chief or it eventually made its way to Detective Graham and angered him, so be it.

Clare wasn't ready to quit her investigation just yet; she still had a few more days. She just didn't have any new ideas on where to look or whom to talk to so she could uncover a helpful clue. If she learned any valuable information between now and the time she had to call it quits, she would add it to her report. Maybe, hopefully, it would motivate someone else to take up the investigation.

The police and sheriff's department were still focused on the current attacks targeting Clare and not on the three-year-old cold case murder of Jessica Barlow. Disappointment weighed heavy on Clare's shoulders and her eyes began to sting with unshed tears. What had she accomplished other than stirring up more trouble and nearly getting herself and Dylan, as well as her dad and Steve, killed? She had to accept that she would likely be plagued with unanswered questions about who killed Jessica and why for the rest of her life. She'd told herself and other people that she would never stop investigating, and in a way that was true. But for now things were coming to a close and there didn't appear to be anything she could do about it. She'd hit a dead end.

Tears in the corners of her eyes spilled down her cheeks and she bowed her head. *Lord, please help me to accept what I need to accept. Not my will, but Yours.*

She grabbed a tissue from a box on the desk and dabbed at her eyes and nose. She glanced at the computer screen and decided this was a good time to rest her eyes for a few minutes before she read through the summary one more time. It would be smart to take a break and then closely review the section where she described Detective Graham's failings as an investigator. The wording of that part was tricky.

A flash of movement outside the window caught Clare's eye and she turned her attention to it. Dylan had returned from working an early patrol shift and she watched him climb out of the ranch truck.

She grimaced at the reminder that his own personal truck had been significantly damaged during the attack on the bridge. Despite Dylan's assurances that his insurance would cover the cost of repairs, Clare was certain he would still be out of pocket for some amount of money and she wanted to make sure she paid him for that.

Yet another reason why she needed to return to work and start earning money again, though she'd have to change jobs soon. Given the physical threats she faced, she'd need to move away from Cedar Lodge as soon as she'd saved enough money. Ending her investigation was no guarantee that the assaults would stop, and following her dream of working as a counselor in Cedar Lodge like her stepmom would not be a possibility as long as the attackers were at large.

She moved closer to the window and watched Dylan head over toward the corral to speak with his dad for a moment as the dogs barked and danced around Dylan's feet. Gazing at him, Clare's heart seemed to expand in her chest. She felt a tenderness for the lawman that she couldn't keep at bay no matter how hard she tried.

Her heart felt heavy in her chest as she remembered the kiss he'd brushed across her forehead yesterday. His care and concern for her were real. Her dawning realization that she actually might be able to endure, and beyond that even thrive in, a marriage to a law enforcement officer was also real. She'd done a lot of thinking about that last night. Danger existed in the world at all times, no matter how cautious a person might be. You couldn't hide from it. And when that danger came in the form of violent criminals, somebody had to step up and stop them. She was grateful to know a man who was willing to do that. But did she have the fortitude to completely give her heart to a man who practically wore a target on his back when he went to work every day? She wasn't completely sure. And she supposed it didn't matter.

This morning, while sipping coffee, she'd heard Dylan on the phone with his childhood friend Henry Walsh, discussing Dylan's plans to begin working private security hostage rescue missions overseas. Clare's heart had dropped when she realized how imminent Dylan's departure might be and how dangerous the job seemed. But for Dylan's sake, because he seemed so enthusiastic about his new adventure, she'd done her best to school her facial expressions and offer a smile when he'd glanced in her direction.

She'd wanted to keep her emotional distance from him at the start of her investigation, but somewhere along the line her feelings had changed. The conversation she'd overheard was evidence that despite whatever he might feel for her, it wasn't enough to deter him from his plans to go work in some faraway place. And to be fair, he'd told her how important that was to him early on.

Looking out at him now through the window, Clare was determined to ignore her painful feelings. She would walk out of the ranch office to the front door and then greet him with a smile on her face. She'd ask if he had an update regarding the search for Madsen and his accomplice and after that she would go back to working on her report.

She headed for the entranceway, trying to dampen her excitement at seeing Dylan. The deputy opened the door and strode in with the happy, energetic canines still at his feet.

"Hey, how's it going?" Dylan asked while setting the gear bag he carried to work on a small bench beside a closet door. "Things got pretty rough yesterday. I hope you've been able to get some rest today."

"I'm fine," Clare said, dismissing his concern. "Any chance you have an update on the search for Madsen?" Realizing she was standing too close to him and sounding too anxious, she took a deep breath and then backed away several steps.

"Unfortunately, no. And believe me, if I'd learned anything significant I would have called or messaged you right away." He spoke with an expression in his eyes that made it clear he was concerned about her.

So much for hiding her feelings about the approaching end of the investigation and the two of them parting ways. But there was no way Clare would tell him that if she seemed "off" right now, it was less because of the investigation or the attacks and more because of *him*. And because of how much she would miss spending time with him.

"I spoke with Sergeant Reid for a few minutes this morning," Dylan added. "He said the fact Madsen and the other guy have managed to evade capture for this long suggests they have accomplices in town. We discussed that a little bit but didn't come to any conclusions."

"I don't have any theories about who could be helping them, either," Clare said.

"I'm going to go change out of my uniform into civilian clothes. After that, you can let me know what investigative work you have planned for this afternoon." He began backing toward the hallway. "I think you should stay here and rest, but it's your call."

"I don't think there's anything else I can do," Clare answered with a shrug.

He slowed down and then stopped. "Are you sure you're okay?"

Yes. No. Apparently not. I don't want you to go to work overseas and disappear from my life forever.

Her concerns about her relationship with him were just more tumbling emotions to add to all the fear and worry and anxiety that already plagued her.

Dear Lord, please give me peace. Your peace.

"I'll be all right." Clare forced some energy into her voice and gestured toward the hallway. "Go change your clothes."

He resumed backing away, but his gaze lingered on her for a few moments before he completely turned around and headed toward the spare bedroom he'd been using.

He was probably grateful that he would be leaving Cedar Lodge soon. He'd be employed alongside a childhood friend doing work that was gratifying to him. Clare wanted that for him even if it meant heartbreak for her. He was a good man who deserved to be happy.

She wandered back to the ranch office, figuring it would be a good idea to print her report and ask Dylan to take a look at it. Especially the part about Detective Graham. That probably needed some adjustment. It was possible she'd been a little too blunt when she was writing it.

"So, what's the plan?" Dylan asked when he stepped into the office a short time later.

Clare pulled the report from the printer and handed it to him. She was about to explain what she was hoping to accomplish with it when her phone rang. She slid the device out of her pocket and looked at the screen. "It's an unknown contact, but the area code and prefix are the Cedar Lodge area."

She accepted the call and put it on speaker. "Hello?"

"Hello, Clare Barlow?" The voice was familiar.

"Yes. Who's this?"

"Rita Carbone."

Clare was so surprised that a beat of silence passed before she could respond and Rita nervously added, "You came into Family Mercantile and wanted to talk with me about your stepmom."

"Thank you so much for calling," Clare said, scrambling to get the words out.

Her stomach twisted with both excitement and dread. She was excited that this might be the moment when she would finally learn what happened to Jessica or at least get a scrap of information that would lead to the cold case being reactivated.

But she was also fearful that she was about to learn some ugly truth regarding her stepmother's final moments that would make Clare's anguish over the vile act even worse than it already was.

Dylan stepped closer to Clare and her phone to better hear the conversation.

"Are you okay, Clare?" Rita's voice came through the speaker. "I heard about what happened to you at your dad's house. That's horrible."

It sounded as if Rita choked up on the final two words and began to cry. Was this sincere emotion, or was Rita faking it? At this point Dylan was compelled to be suspicious of virtually everyone.

"I'm all right." Clare spoke cautiously and turned to Dylan with her eyebrows raised in a questioning expression.

Good, she's not taking things at face value, either.

"I feel bad for what you're going through." Rita broke into tears again before clearing her throat. "It's all my fault."

"Why?" Clare kept a calm tone, though anxiety was written in her creased brow and tense posture. "How are you involved in the attacks? What's your connection?" She glanced at Dylan before adding, "I think you should talk to the police."

"*No!* Not yet, anyway."

Why not the police? Unease had Dylan questioning whether Rita might be criminally liable for something. Or could she be afraid of someone within the police department, like maybe Detective Graham?

In the background on Rita's end of the call Dylan heard a female voice say, "Don't do anything until you're ready."

"Who is that?" Clare asked. "Who is there with you?"

"My cousin, Libby. You met her at the store."

Dylan's mind raced. Had Rita confided in Libby and now her cousin was encouraging her to come forward with what Rita knew? Was that the reason Rita had decided to call now instead of earlier? Was Libby somehow also involved? He didn't have nearly enough information yet to put together the pieces of the puzzle, but that didn't stop him from beginning to assess the little bit of new information that came with this call.

"Rita," Clare said. "Please, tell me what you have to say."

There was indecipherable whispering between Rita

and Libby on their end of the call. "What if you're using some kind of recording device and you'll use this against me?" Rita's tone turned suspicious.

"I assure you I'm not recording this," Clare said. "But if you'd like I can come to the store and you can tell me what you have to say in person."

"*No!* You can't do that. Don't try to contact me at the store. In fact, don't come to the store ever again." Rita sounded on the verge of panic.

Dylan and Clare exchanged glances. Was Rita going to hang up without giving any information at all? "I'll stay away from the store," Clare said. "I promise."

There was a gap of silence with some more whispering in the background. Clare bit her lip and Dylan rested a hand on her shoulder. He could only imagine what she was feeling as she hoped to finally get the information she wanted so badly while Rita wavered on telling her.

"We think it would be best to meet away from the store," Rita finally said.

"'*We?*'" Clare asked.

"Libby is coming, too. We want to meet at the Cedar Lodge Nature Center. In an hour."

The center was atop a forested hill outside of town and a short walk from a scenic overlook of the Meadowlark River. Dylan began calculating the measures he would need to put in place ahead of time to make certain the meeting was secure.

"There are tables on the grass outside the snack bar area where we can sit and talk," Rita said. "We'll be able to make sure there's no one nearby listening in."

"You've really thought this through," Clare commented.

"I have. And don't bring your sheriff's deputy friend. Like I said, I'm not ready to talk to the police, yet."

Dylan's stomach fisted. There was no way Clare would go to this meeting unprotected and without him. He leaned over and tapped the mute button on Clare's phone. "We need time to position surveillance in case this is a setup. Tell her you can meet her in *two* hours."

Clare unmuted her phone and glanced at the time. "It's nearly three o'clock. I'll meet you at five."

Dylan heard more whispering on the other end of the call. "No," Rita said. "*One* hour. I'm not going to give you extra time to get cops up there to listen in or spy on us or whatever."

Clare sighed. "How do I know I can trust you?"

"How do I know I can trust *you*?"

"You don't have to do this," Libby said to her cousin on their end of the call. "You can change your mind."

"No," Clare quickly interjected. "I appreciate you agreeing to talk to me. I'll see you in *one* hour."

Clare disconnected the call and turned to Dylan, her face flushed. After tucking her phone in her pocket, she ran her hands through her hair and took a deep breath. "Okay, well, I guess this is it. Looks like I'm finally going to get that piece of information I've been looking for to get Jessica's murder investigation back on track." Her voice shook with nerves. "I've got to get going." A worried expression crossed her face. "But I don't have my car here."

"I'll drive you."

She shook her head. "Rita said not to bring you. If she sees you, she won't talk to me."

"I'm sorry, but that's a risk we're going to have to take. We don't know what kind of situation you might be walking into." He grabbed his phone, went through his contacts and sent Officer Kris Volker's phone number to Clare. "Volker is on patrol until later this evening. I'll ask him to stay near the nature center while we're there. If things go sideways and something happens to me, call Kris for help. He'll get there the fastest and he'll alert the rest of the cavalry."

Clare stared at him with fear in her eyes. "I don't want anything bad to happen to you."

He shrugged. "Not everything is under our control. And I don't want anything bad to happen to *you*, either. That's why I'm coming along."

Clare got to her feet and tapped at her phone screen to put Kris Volker's number into her contacts.

Dylan considered what they were heading into. Maybe this was a legitimate meeting and Rita really did have some information she wanted to share. Or maybe she was only pretending she wanted to help because someone else was forcing her to and it would all lead to another attack. But Clare was desperate for details on the events surrounding the murder of her stepmother and he understood why she was determined to go despite the potential danger.

Dylan would attend this meeting even though Rita didn't want him there. If that made Rita cancel her plans to speak with Clare, so be it. With so many unknowns swirling around, there was no way Dylan would leave Clare unprotected.

THIRTEEN

Clare sat beside Dylan as they drove up to the crest of Cedar Hill and parked in the nature center lot. Under normal circumstances, Clare's attention would be focused on the natural beauty of the pine and cedar forest surrounding them. Instead, she twisted her hands in her lap and tried to ignore the knot in her stomach while her gaze roamed over the parking lot and she peered at the other vehicles. She was watchful of the people climbing out of them and strolling toward the center's main building and official entrance.

Maybe she and Dylan should have asked for official law enforcement backup during this meeting and accepted the risk that Rita might see them and be scared off. But there hadn't been much time and there was no guarantee the city police or county sheriff's department would have assigned someone, anyway. This was a simple meeting that offered no discernible threat and broke no law.

Dylan turned off the truck's engine and then reached for the handgun he'd put in the glove box. Their gazes connected for the span of a few heartbeats and he reached over to brush his finger along her jawline. "Stay close."

Clare nodded nervously as she reached up to rest her hand atop his for a moment. "Believe me, I will." She might be the intended target in all of the attacks, but Dylan's determination to stay by her side put him in peril, as well. Despite his demonstrated competence and skill, she was afraid for him as much as for herself.

He had a place in her heart, there was no denying that. But he'd told her directly that he didn't want a personal relationship with her and she'd heard for herself that he still intended to follow his career ambitions even though they would take him far away.

She gave herself these few seconds to acknowledge what she felt and at the same time to commit to letting him go. He was a good man and she wanted a happy and fulfilling life for him, even if that meant they went their separate ways. Assuming this meeting turned out to be helpful to her investigation. And that they didn't get killed.

They got out of the truck and their footsteps crunched atop the loose gravel until they reached the grassy hilltop, where the cluster of city park services buildings began. The local history museum was situated to the left. The actual nature center, with its exhibits and bookstore and presentation hall, was directly in front.

They headed into the center, bypassing several displays of local flora and fauna with attached descriptions, and headed directly for the smoked glass exit door at the rear. As they approached it, Dylan held out a staying hand, cautioning Clare to stay back until he could take a look and make certain it was safe for her to step outside.

The fear and anxiety of the last few days seemed to peak and then crash over Clare while she stood waiting. What if they were walking into a trap? What if her decision to come to this meeting got her and Dylan killed?

This constant exposure to danger couldn't go on any longer. Not even for a few more days until she went back to work. She couldn't continue to put people she cared about in situations that could get them killed. Whatever information she obtained today, she would turn over to the police and then she would let it all go.

Risking her own life and the lives of people she loved—there was no denying that included Dylan—for the mere *possibility* of learning new details about a tragic event in the past that couldn't be changed made no sense. She understood that now in a way that she hadn't before. She *had* to trust God to establish His own reckoning over what had happened to Jessica. An earthly system of justice was well and good and necessary. But it was not perfect and it could not be all-encompassing.

Clare remained inside the building, hands curled into tense fists that she dropped to her side, until Dylan returned to let her know the situation outside the door looked safe.

They strode across a patio, threading their way between several people seated in Adirondack chairs arranged around a firepit. The snack bar was located beyond the patio on a grassy plot of land. The building was a simple arrangement with two walk-up windows for purchases. A half dozen picnic tables were placed nearby with some of them in the shade offered by trees and others in the sunlight.

"I don't see Rita," Clare said, scanning the picnic tables as they drew closer. But after a few more steps the view around the end of the snack bar opened up and she spotted a table significantly farther from the snack bar building. There was a woman seated at the table, but she wasn't the person Clare most wanted to see.

"That's Rita's cousin, Libby," Clare said. She looked around. "Where's Rita?"

Dylan shook his head. "I don't see her."

Libby beckoned them toward her. "Rita went to wash her hands," Libby said as they approached her. "She'll be right back."

Clare and Dylan took a seat on the bench opposite Libby. And then Libby lifted the left side of her jacket and exposed a gun in her right hand that was pointed directly at Clare. "Don't scream," Libby said quietly. "Don't look around and don't move until I tell you to. If you do any of those things, I'll shoot you right now. I have no reason to keep you alive."

The blood drained from Clare's face and she couldn't breathe. She finally forced in some air, but it felt as if her lungs were encased in concrete

"What?" she finally sputtered. "What is happening? Where is Rita?"

Libby ignored the question and stared at Clare through malice-filled eyes. Her lips pressed into a frown that radiated contempt.

"We've walked into a trap." Dylan bit out the words. "What do you plan to do with us?" he asked Libby.

He shifted his weight slightly and Libby tilted her head. "Reach for the pistol I'm sure you're carrying, Deputy, and I'll kill Clare right here and now. While I'm doing that, my partner will kill you before you can do anything about it."

Partner? Did she mean Rita? Clare cautiously shifted her gaze to search for the sable-haired store clerk while at the same time remembering Libby's warning to her not to look around.

"There are plenty of witnesses nearby," Dylan said, his voice tense but otherwise calm. "Do you really think you'll get away with killing us?"

"Everybody will hit the ground when they hear gunfire," Libby said. "By the time they look up, I'll have disappeared into the woods. I'm not worried about video because I didn't walk through the nature center building to get here and there are no security cameras aimed at this particular spot."

"What do you want?" Clare asked.

Libby's sour smile vanished. "Get up. Both of you hold your hands away from your body. I don't want the cop reaching for his gun. And after all you've been through, Clare, I wouldn't be surprised if you were packing a weapon now, too."

Dear Lord, please help us. With her gaze locked on the barrel of Libby's gun, Clare moved her hands as Libby demanded and awkwardly climbed from the bench seat and stood behind it. Dylan did the same.

Libby had also gotten to her feet. "We're going to head into the forest behind us, just like any of the other nature lovers who are out here today." She glanced at Dylan. "My gun is going to be pointed at Clare, just so you know. You try anything and she'll die as a result."

"But *why* are you doing this?" Clare's increasing sense of panic was evident in her voice.

"Move now or die right here," Libby responded, ignoring the question.

"Let's do as she says," Dylan said to Clare.

Libby gave a slight nod. "Wise choice."

Clare and Dylan walked into the forest with Libby behind them, giving directions on which way they should go. She didn't want them following any of the established trails that originated at the nature center, but instead had them step off into the dense woods. Clare hoped they would come across other off-trail hikers so she could somehow communicate a request for help, but that didn't happen. She and Dylan were alone with a woman determined to kill them.

Lord, I know You are with me.

The skin on the back of Clare's neck itched in dread of the burn of a bullet.

What was Libby waiting for? Her accomplice to show up? And would Rita be that accomplice, or had Rita also been a target in this deadly setup?

They reached a decline in the forest floor. Clare stepped downward onto a patch of damp pine needles that shifted under her weight and sent her sliding toward a tree.

"Run!" Dylan shouted.

Clare sensed more than saw a sudden flurry of movement beside her. Confused and physically off-balance, she grabbed the tree to steady herself and then turned to help Dylan.

Bang!

The gunshot tore at Clare's heart despite it not having struck her physically and she didn't know what to do. Fearful that throwing herself into the melee could distract Dylan and put him at further risk, she forced herself to do as he'd instructed and just *ran*.

Libby had managed to fire off a shot before Dylan whirled around and knocked the gun out of her hand. He reached for his own weapon secured at the small of his back when a sudden weight fell on him, pushing him down and pinning his arms at his sides while his face was shoved into the dirt.

As the unseen attacker grabbed Dylan's gun from his waistband, the deputy spun free of the assailant's grasp and kicked him in the chest, sending the man stumbling backward.

Madsen's accomplice. Dylan had caught glimpses of the perp's face in prior attacks and he also recognized the hoodie. So where was Madsen?

While Dylan shoved himself to his feet, the accomplice sprang forward and poked the barrel of Dylan's gun into his face. The man stared at him through pale blue eyes, his expression strangely impassive. But then a professional killer wouldn't necessarily have much emotion tied up in his assaults. It would just be another job. So, like Madsen, this creep must be a hired gun.

"Want me to kill him?" the criminal asked.

Libby had recovered her weapon. "Not yet."

Dylan glanced around. At least it appeared Clare had gotten away. He hoped she was still running, as fast and hard as she could. *Thank You, Lord.*

But he'd expected to see Rita at some point and he still hadn't. "Did Rita set us up?" he asked Libby, attempting to buy time engaging her in conversation while he figured out a way to escape.

Libby shook her head. "Don't worry about my cousin. This will be the last time her good intentions get her into trouble."

The accomplice moved closer to Dylan. "Put up your hands."

"Where's your fellow hired killer Kirk Madsen?"

The gunman offered a cold smile. "He's chasing down your girlfriend, Clare, as we speak. You didn't think she'd actually gotten away, did you?"

Dylan's stomach dropped. The accomplice and Madsen must have been following them and staying out of sight from the time they'd left the nature center.

"Take out your phone and call Clare," Libby said. She'd

gentled her tone and features, making it apparent how skilled she was at hiding her real self.

Did Rita know the true, criminal Libby, or had she been fooled by her cousin?

"Get your sweetheart to come back here," Libby continued. "Tell her that you managed to get away from us and everything's fine. Do that, and we'll make things quick and painless for the both of you. Otherwise, well, you can probably guess what the other option is. Something much more unpleasant."

"No!" Dylan refused to give up hope that Clare would escape unharmed. She was a smart, resourceful woman. Even with a professional hit man hot on her heels, Clare had a chance of getting away.

"Fine," Libby said. "I'll call her on Rita's phone. She'll recognize the number and she'll answer."

Don't pick up, Dylan thought, as if through sheer force of will he could make Clare realize that remaining silent in the forest was her best and safest option. The phone ringing alone could give away her location, but if these creeps also got her talking it would be that much easier for Madsen to find her.

Libby pulled a phone from her pocket and tapped the screen a couple of times.

Please let the call not go through. There were spots all around the town of Cedar Lodge where phone connectivity was absent. He hoped this was one of them.

In the quiet of the forest he could hear Clare's phone ringing in the near distance. She hadn't gone very far at all. "Hello? Rita?"

Dylan's heart sank. *"Get off the phone and run!"* he shouted. Ignoring the gun pointed at him, he moved closer to the phone in Libby's hand and shouted again. *"Madsen's after you! He'll hear you talking and find you!"*

"Dylan! Are you—"

The call dropped midsentence and the deputy's heart practically fell out of his chest.

Had Clare ended the call intentionally, or did the sudden disconnect mean that Madsen had found her?

FOURTEEN

Clare choked back a sob. She'd been in the middle of asking Dylan if he was all right when the meaning of what he'd said sank in and she'd immediately disconnected. Now she crouched behind a tree with her phone muted, hand to her mouth, trying not to make a sound as tears threatened to overtake her.

The criminals had Dylan, and Clare couldn't know for certain if he was still alive. Maybe they'd done something to him to shut him up after he'd called out to her.

She looked around fearfully. What if Madsen had already found her? Or maybe he hadn't spotted her yet, but he was close by. She'd hidden between a tree and a bush and right now she couldn't see much of anything beyond leaves and twigs and the pine needles on low-hanging branches.

What should she do? Find her way back to the nature center to get assistance, or stay hidden and wait? Did she dare make the sounds it would take to call 911 for help? And could emergency responders even arrive in time?

Kris Volker! Dylan said he would ask his cop friend to patrol the area near the nature center. That would place Kris somewhere along the two-lane highway they'd turned off to get to the parking lot near the top of Cedar Hill.

Clare gripped her phone, afraid to use it but also afraid that if she didn't use it, Dylan would die. It would take too long to text Volker about what had happened, never mind directions on how to get to the place where she'd last seen Dylan. Beyond that, she didn't dare focus her gaze on the phone screen when she needed to keep her eyes on her soundings and watch for Madsen.

Hoping that she was making the right decision, Clare found Kris's number in her directory, made sure she had the volume turned down low and tapped the screen for a phone call.

"Volker."

"They've got Dylan!" Clare whispered.

"Where are you guys?"

"We're not together. He told me to run and I did." Guilt for leaving Dylan behind pulled at her, but she did her best to shove her regret aside. She gave Kris a quick description of what had happened and where she'd last seen Dylan.

He asked a few questions to get clarity on the situation.

Clare's body was tense with fear, and while speaking to Kris she did her best to be attentive to her surroundings. Wind swirled in the treetops and sent leaves rustling, all normal sounds though they put her nerves on edge. She heard the occasional chirp of a bird or chattering of a squirrel.

But then she heard something different. Like maybe a footfall atop a pile of dried pine needles.

"I think Madsen found me," she whispered with her lips against the phone and her lungs so tight with fear she could barely speak.

"I'm already on my way," Volker said at the other end of the call.

Clare disconnected and held her breath, listening as carefully as she could. Her hands trembled and she nearly dropped her phone.

"Clare," a male voice called out. It was Kirk Madsen. "I told you that you should have just let things go with Jessica's murder when we met in Garnet Park. Your cop friend Deputy Ruiz is about to meet the same fate as your stepmother. Come out from wherever you're hiding and talk to me. Do that and you could save the deputy's life."

Fear mixed sickeningly with dread as Clare desperately tried to figure out what to do. If she came out from hiding, Madsen would shoot her on sight. That was what he'd been hired to do, and he had to be anxious to finish the job. But if she stayed put, he would find her eventually.

She had to get away, but how long would it take for him to catch up with her? Beyond that, could she live with herself if she kept running while she knew Dylan was in danger? He was a lawman and an army veteran and more than capable. But he wasn't invincible. No one was. And he'd given Clare so much help and support without asking for anything in return.

She made her decision and crept as quickly and quietly as she could, away from her hiding place and back in the direction where she'd last seen Dylan. It didn't take long until she heard voices. Volker, maybe? Her heart leaped at the possibility that the cop was already there with fellow officers.

But a few seconds later she realized it was not Volker but rather Dylan and Libby talking in tense tones along with the unidentified male voice Clare had heard stalking her and Dylan in the aftermath of the bridge attack.

Crouching and moving forward, Clare pushed aside a

tree branch until she could see Dylan. He didn't appear to have been shot, and she was grateful for that.

Something snapped in the forest behind her. She spun around and through the foliage caught a brief flash of movement. Kirk Madsen wasn't far behind her.

Clare had to act. She would run directly toward Dylan and the two criminals. If she could surprise and knock down Libby, Dylan could take care of the unidentified guy who was pointing a gun at him. She had no idea what would happen with Madsen lurking nearby, but she couldn't wait until she had a perfect plan to actually *do* something. It was too late for that.

She took a deep breath and then darted out, taking Dylan and the criminals by surprise. She threw herself at Libby, hurling the woman to the ground with enough force to knock the gun from her hand. Clare stretched to pick it up and then scrambled to her feet and pointed it at her.

Dylan took advantage of Clare's surprise sudden appearance and attacked the unidentified criminal, wrestling him to the ground and finally landing a punch to the jaw that left the man stunned and unmoving. Dylan pulled the gun from the creep's hand and another from the man's waistband.

Bang! Bang!

Madsen had reached the edge of the small clearing and was firing as he strode forward, determined to kill Dylan and Clare.

Dylan moved to shield Clare's body with his own as he returned fire at Madsen. The hit man jerked as if struck, and stumbled backward into the woods.

"Dylan!" a voice shouted from the direction of the nature center. It was accompanied by the sounds of several people running toward them.

"Kris! Over here!"

Kris Volker appeared through the woods, accompanied by three other cops.

"Be careful," Dylan called out. He pointed toward the edge of the clearing. "Madsen's over there somewhere and he's armed. I might have shot him down or he might have run away, I'm not sure which."

Volker gestured at two officers, who took off in search of Madsen.

Clare kept her gun pointed at Libby as she asked Volker, "How did you find us so fast?"

"Your directions on your general location were good. After that we followed the sound of gunfire."

The two cops came out of the woods with Madsen in custody. The hit man appeared to have been shot in the upper arm, but he was not bleeding severely and was able to walk. He hollered threats at Clare and Dylan, which were echoed by Madsen's accomplice. The accomplice had gathered his wits enough to push himself to his feet, at which point he was handcuffed by one of the cops.

"We need to get these goons out of here," Kris said as he made sure the three criminals were properly secured. They all headed toward the nature center and its adjacent parking lot.

Clare, shaky with fatigue and the sudden adrenaline drop, was frustrated with the unanswered questions that still lingered. The criminals were in custody, yet she *still* had no idea what all of the events leading up to this event meant or how they were connected to Jessica.

"Who murdered my stepmom?" she demanded of Libby, walking beside her. "Was it you?"

Libby glowered. "Talk to my lawyer."

"And where's Rita?"

Libby just scowled and shook her head.

Instead of heading out through the nature center building, the cops led their perps down the grassy area beside it. There were already patrol cars in the parking lot and Clare watched two more vehicles arrive. Volker tapped his collar mic to confirm they had three in custody.

Across the parking lot, Clare spotted a familiar-looking man running away toward two vehicles in a far corner. He glanced in her direction, and she realized she'd seen him before, when she and Dylan were at Family Mercantile.

"That's Rita and Libby's uncle!" she called out. "What's he doing here?" Fully aware that neither Dylan nor the cops around her could give her an answer, Clare started running toward the man. "Hey! Max Durand! *Stop!*"

Max sped up to get into a vehicle. Dylan raced past Clare to stop him. Clare was only a few steps behind Dylan and she caught up with the deputy as he grabbed hold of Max and began questioning him. She turned to the car beside Max's, and saw another familiar face. Rita Carbone. She looked unconscious.

Clare yelled for help and a cop hustled over and broke a car window so he could get a door open and reach Rita. He felt for a pulse and called out, "She's alive."

Dylan handed off Max to one of the cops to be officially detained. Volker was already on the radio asking for emergency medical services for Rita.

Paramedic Cole Webb responded over the radio that he was on his way.

Clare burst into tears. Her life had become a frustrating nightmare where all she had was questions and she never seemed to get any answers. She realized she should be concerned about Rita and not just herself, but she couldn't help being upset. She was so tired.

Strong arms wrapped around her and Dylan pulled her close to his chest. She leaned into him, feeling his heartbeat and drawing strength from the warmth of his arms engulfing her.

He smoothed her hair. "That was some counterattack you launched back there, running out of the woods like that. You even scared me a little."

Somehow Clare managed to laugh through her tears.

"It'll be okay," Dylan said, gently pressing his lips to her forehead. "Even if you don't get the answers you're looking for, you'll survive. Somehow, you'll manage to find peace."

It was as if he'd read her thoughts. But why was she surprised? It felt as if the two of them had been in tune with one another from the start.

Clare knew they had no future together, that his plans didn't include her. Nevertheless, she also knew for certain that she *could* fall in love with a man who faced danger on a daily basis. Because she already had.

The heartache that pierced her was sharp and real. She longed to ask him to reconsider leaving the country. But she'd already asked so much of Deputy Dylan Ruiz. He'd given her the help she'd needed and then some. He'd offered her friendship and courage and the strength to carry on. The least she could do was let him go to create the life he wanted, with adrenaline-fueled, life-or-death situations on a daily basis, without making things more difficult for him.

She wouldn't see much of him after today. A debrief session at the sheriff's department where maybe they would finally get the mystery of the murder of Jessica unraveled. And after that it would all be over.

That being the case, Clare gave in to the impulse to lift

her head, offer a smile to the handsome deputy who gave
her a smile in return, and then plant a kiss on his lips.

Dylan immediately kissed her back, his lips warm and
lingering, while his hands gently pressed the small of her
back. For the moment, at least, the concerns that had been
hounding Clare, for so long, quieted. She would worry
about the pain of missing Dylan later, after they went their
separate ways. Right now, she would enjoy whatever time
they had together.

Dylan stayed by Clare's side as they waited in the sheriff's department conference room. In the hours since they'd
arrived, he'd taken hold of her hand several times and
she'd squeezed his in return. His memory of that kiss in
the parking lot was something he would keep forever. But
for now he couldn't stop wondering, was it just the joy of
the moment that fueled her kiss or was it something more?

In Dylan's case, that kiss was about something *much*
more. He'd fallen in love with Clare, there was no longer
any denying it. But she'd made it clear she didn't want a
relationship with a law enforcement officer because she
was afraid of the danger he would regularly face. Her
worry, originally triggered by the murder of her stepmother, was likely twice as strong after what the two of
them had just been through.

Meanwhile, Dylan had reached the point where he
knew that hard-charging around the world with Henry
Walsh and his private security operatives was not what he
needed to fill the well of dissatisfaction in his life. He'd
noticed earlier that being around Clare had calmed that
nagging sense that something important was missing from
his life. He'd tried to convince himself that the peace in
his heart had come about simply because he was busy.

He'd been deluding himself, he probably knew that then, but he *definitely* knew that now. It was hard to admit he'd fallen in love. He was a take-action, in-control kind of guy and this was something he couldn't control. And the funny thing was, even though a part of him still whispered that he hadn't earned the right to settle down with a family and be happy, a stronger and faith-filled part of him told him it would be wise to graciously accept the gift God was offering him.

He was willing to do that, but even so, Dylan couldn't see giving up his job as a sheriff's deputy. This recent altercation confirmed that there were vicious people in the world and the potential victims who were targeted needed someone to protect them. Dylan was the kind of guy who could do that. His sense of self-respect *demanded* that he do it.

So where did that leave himself and Clare?

"The interrogation that's going on right now could take all night," Dylan said quietly, turning to Clare in the chair beside him.

The perps who were arrested at the nature center were being questioned. Meanwhile, through the glass wall of the conference room they'd seen Homicide Detective Anthony Graham brought in by a sheriff's deputy. The detective hadn't been handcuffed, so he likely wasn't under arrest, but he'd looked grim. Police Chief Ellis had also shown up and he appeared to be working alongside Sheriff Finley.

"Maybe I should take you back to the ranch so you can get some rest," Dylan said. Clare had called her dad and brother to let them know the assailants had been captured and it was safe to return home, but they weren't planning to head back to Cedar Lodge until tomorrow morning.

Beyond the practical reason of taking Clare back to the ranch so she wouldn't be alone after a traumatic event, Dylan simply liked the idea of having her there. He had his own home to return to eventually, but he wasn't ready to let go of the opportunity to be around her. He liked watching her sip coffee in the morning with that messy bun on her head. He liked seeing her when he returned to the ranch after working a shift on patrol. It lifted his spirits and brought a lightness to his heart that he hadn't felt in a long time. She was strong and courageous and a woman he could see himself loving for a lifetime. But he wasn't sure he would ever have that chance, so he wanted to spend as much time with her as he could before she moved out.

Clare offered him a tired smile. "Obviously I'll be perfectly safe sitting here, so why don't you go back to the ranch if you're tired."

He shook his head. "I'm not going without you."

Her eyes widened slightly, and then her cheeks turned red before she looked away. Dylan was fairly certain his own cheeks were red, too. She did that to him.

He'd just taken a sip of the strong coffee he'd gotten from the break room when he heard voices outside the conference room. A door opened and a stream of cops and lawyers from the county prosecutor's office headed into the squad room from the interrogation area.

Sheriff Finley stepped into the conference room and beckoned Dylan and Clare. "We've got some information for you, Clare. Come with me."

Clare was on her feet in an instant and Dylan walked with her to the sheriff's office, where Chief Ellis was already waiting.

"Which of them murdered my stepmother and why?" Clare blurted out.

The sheriff turned to her, a sympathetic expression on her face, and said, "Libby Santos shot and killed Jessica Barlow. The 'why' is going to take a minute to explain." She gestured at a chair. "Please sit down."

"Let me start by offering my personal apology," Police Chief Ellis said to Clare after everyone was seated.

Clare took Dylan's hand and the deputy offered a quick, silent prayer hoping that what they were about to learn wouldn't be too much for Clare to handle. She wanted answers, but it might be painful to hear them.

"Homicide Detective Anthony Graham has been placed on leave while we negotiate an end to his employment with the Cedar Lodge Police Department." The police chief cleared his throat. "He has confessed to intentionally under-investigating your stepmother's murder case because he was afraid his own son, who had a notable criminal history at that point, was somehow involved in it. More recently, when you rightfully pushed to have your stepmother's case moved to the active side of the board, the detective was fearful that his own lack of due diligence would be discovered. So he was the one who left the threatening notes for you early on. But when you were actually physically attacked at the cabin, Graham stopped leaving the notes."

"And Libby?" Clare prompted.

"We need to start with Rita Carbone," Sheriff Finley said, sitting on the edge of her desk. "Detectives just concluded an interview with Rita at the hospital where she'll be staying overnight for observation. She was unconscious in the car because she'd unknowingly ingested a strong sedative in a cup of coffee given to her by Libby."

The sheriff cleared her throat. "The detectives learned from Rita that her family's store has not been doing well for some time, which is not a complete surprise. Her uncle Max Durand, who'd bought out the other family members thinking he could turn things around, was angry that his plans hadn't worked and that there wasn't enough money coming in for him to enjoy the lifestyle he'd imagined he would have. So he began his own enterprise on the side, involving drug dealing plus credit card skimming. He kept the department store open to maintain his image as a legitimate businessman."

"He ran an actual criminal organization?" Dylan asked, stunned. He looked back and forth between the sheriff and the police chief. "Did anyone know about this?"

The sheriff shook her head. "We were aware of increased drug dealing and credit card skimming over the last few years, but we hadn't connected any of it to Max Durand. To be honest, we didn't even suspect him."

"Did my stepmom somehow learn about this?" Clare asked.

The sheriff nodded. "A pair of criminal competitors learned what Max Durand was doing and tried to move in on his action. Durand had them killed. We're still working out plea deals to get specific, detailed information about that. Rita overheard conversations about the murders between her uncle and some of his criminal employees and realized Max was responsible for the killings. She felt like she had to do something about it, but she was afraid to go to the police. She told her cousin, Libby, about what she'd learned, and believed Libby was as shocked and appalled as she was."

"But Libby was actually in on the criminal business?"

"Yes."

"Did Rita tell my stepmom about this when they met for lunch?"

"Not exactly. Rita talked to your stepmom a lot at church. With guilt weighing on her and confusion over what she should do, Rita met Jessica for lunch to get a feel for whether she could trust Jessica with the truth and perhaps get some advice on how to handle the situation."

"So at that point they weren't talking about anything criminal at all?" Dylan interjected.

"They weren't." The sheriff shook her head then turned her attention back to Clare. "Rita ultimately decided she could trust your stepmother, but she didn't want to discuss sensitive information with her in a public place like a restaurant. She contacted Jessica after the meeting at Mimi's Bistro and asked if they could meet in an out-of-the-way place like Garnet Park."

Clare took a deep breath, appearing to prepare herself for what she would hear next.

The sheriff paused. "Are you certain you want to know what happened after that?"

"Yes," Clare whispered.

"Rita believed Libby felt the same way she did, that she, too, was horrified by what their uncle Max was doing. So Rita told Libby about her plans to meet Jessica in the park and tell her about the criminal activities and then get her advice on how to relay that information to the police."

"So, she wanted to do the right thing," Clare said.

"Yes, and Libby pretended to be sympathetic, but then she gave Max a heads-up on what Rita was doing. Max had Libby follow Rita. Upon arrival at Garnet Park, Libby contacted Max and he quickly drove over to meet her."

"So Max went there with the intent to murder Jessica," Dylan said.

The sheriff nodded. "Keep in mind that Rita never actually saw Libby in the park," Finley continued. "Rita was speaking with your stepmom by the oak tree when Max showed up, pointed a gun at Jessica, and told her to stay where she was while he forced Rita to leave with him."

"So Rita didn't actually witness the killing," Clare said softly to herself.

"Correct," the sheriff said. "Rita and Max were in the parking lot when Rita heard the gunshots back in the area where they'd left Jessica. She could guess what had happened, though she assumed one of Max's criminal employees had snuck into the area and committed the murder. She had no idea the shooter was her cousin, Libby."

Dylan shook his head, unnerved at how easily Libby had hidden her vicious criminal nature, even from her own cousin.

"Max figured that killing Jessica this way would not only silence her for good so the police wouldn't find out about his criminal enterprise, but that it would also terrify Rita into keeping her mouth shut. His plan worked for three years, until you started talking to people about the murder and Rita's conscience started bothering her."

Clare sat with her eyes closed for a moment.

Dylan couldn't imagine how it felt for her to absorb everything she'd just heard. He reached beside him to rest his hand atop hers.

Clare opened her eyes. "If all of this happened in the park, why do you think Jessica's scarf was found in town close to her office?"

The sheriff shrugged. "There's no sign that it was related to the attack at all. My best guess is that she simply dropped it at some point and the wind blew it the short distance down the street where it got caught in the shrubs.

And then, as you know, after some time it was discovered, and that prompted you to begin your investigation."

"How were you able to get so much information?" Dylan asked the sheriff.

"Rita told us a lot of it, which will likely result in lesser charges being pursued against her by the city prosecutor. Plus, we've got a few people connected to Max Durand's criminal enterprise anxious to work out a plea deal as quickly as they can. We got their names from Rita and sent officers to talk to them. They're scared they'll be going to prison for a long time."

"Why were they so anxious to kill *me*?" Clare asked. "They'd gotten away with the murder for three years. Why not just stay quiet?"

"You were so dogged about getting the murder investigation reactivated that Max was convinced you had some kind of actual evidence. Or that Jessica had learned the details of his operation and told you about it."

Clare looked stunned. "He thought I *knew* something about who might have killed her and why?"

The sheriff nodded. "He couldn't believe you would put so much effort into trying to solve her case, which is what he figured you were *really* doing, unless you had some solid information to start with."

"So is Kirk Madsen part of his gang?" Dylan asked.

"Not exactly. Madsen had done some criminal work for Durand in the past, so Max hired him to get rid of Clare. When Clare turned out to be more of a challenge than Madsen expected, he brought his accomplice on board to help get the job done."

Clare sat quietly for a moment. "Jessica was willing to help somebody and she ended up paying for that with her life."

The sheriff sighed. "Unfortunately, yes."

"Thank you," Clare said, looking exhausted as she got to her feet. "I finally have my answers, and I'm grateful. I look forward to seeing the criminals responsible for Jessica's death brought to justice." She took a deep breath and rolled her shoulders. "I'll let my dad and my brother know what we've learned."

Dylan stood up beside her. He wrapped an arm around her shoulder since she looked as if she was about to collapse.

"You'll keep me updated as the prosecution progresses?" Clare asked the sheriff.

"Absolutely."

They started out of the office and Dylan pulled Clare a little closer. She leaned into him and it felt as if they belonged together.

"Shall I take you back to the ranch?" he asked, since she hadn't answered that question earlier.

"Sure."

At least they would be together a little while longer.

FIFTEEN

Clare opened her eyes and blinked at the bright sunlight pouring down on her through a gap between the curtains in the bedroom window.

She'd been exhausted by the time she and Dylan had arrived at the Ruiz ranch late last night and she'd gone to bed almost immediately. Despite hearing the details of her stepmother's murder, Clare had fallen into a deep, sound sleep.

The heartless act she'd heard detailed was three years in the past, and now that she'd had her questions answered and the perpetrators were facing justice, she could accept what had happened and find peace in knowing she'd done everything she could for her beloved stepmother.

Clare would never get over the horrific loss, but she could now find a way to weave that experience into her life and move on as she strove to make the most of every moment that she had left to live. Jessica would have wanted that. Clare had no doubt about it.

Thank You, Lord. She had so much to be grateful for, despite the losses she'd endured in life. And gratitude was where she wanted to focus her thoughts as she moved forward. She yawned, sat up in bed and stretched. Her gaze moved to the cute cat-shaped wall clock and was startled to see that it was nearly ten in the morning. On her previous mornings at the ranch she'd woken up well before sunrise, her sleep having been fitful and not particularly restorative, as she'd been troubled by uncertainty and anxiety.

Now, finally, her life felt like it was back in balance.

Except for the part where she'd fallen in love with a certain brown-eyed lawman whose intense gaze and slow smile made her weak in the knees. And when it came to that kiss in the nature center parking lot…well, good thing she'd had his strong shoulders to hang on to or she might have collapsed.

But physical attraction alone wasn't enough. She had enough life experience to know that. Even the buzzing romantic feeling that had stirred her heart while Dylan's lips were pressed to hers yesterday afternoon wouldn't sustain a relationship, let alone a marriage.

Back when she was a teen, Clare's dad had told her about the over-the-top attraction he and Clare's biological mother, Margot, had felt for each other when they met and quickly married. He'd told her as a warning, of course. Initial intensity of emotion was not the only thing to consider when looking toward building a future with someone. Ultimately, Margot and her dad had been two people with very different values, wanting to live two very different lives, and that had torn their marriage apart.

Clare knew that she and Dylan shared similar values with one another, including a commitment to their faith. But she wanted to stay in Cedar Lodge, at least for the near future. It was important for her to be around her teenage brother as he grew up. She also wanted to attend as many criminal proceedings as she could until the killers who'd ended Jessica's life were convicted and sent to prison. And she planned to build a career as a counselor in the community.

She didn't want to feel as if she were hanging on to Dylan and holding him back from the work that would bring fulfillment to his life, so she would not ask him to stay. Clare's dad had begged Margot not to leave town when Clare was a young girl, but ultimately that hadn't done any good. Her biological mother had stayed a little longer, but then the fights had resumed and ultimately she'd left, anyway.

Clare would not put herself in that same position with Dylan, pleading with him not to go.

She threw back the covers and rolled out of bed. The house sounded quiet. Dylan's dad was likely outside working and his mom was probably out there, too.

No doubt Dylan was out on patrol somewhere in the county. The thought that she wouldn't see him again before he moved out of town made her sad, but what could she do? He didn't normally live on the ranch. He had his own place and he'd just moved to his parents' home temporarily to offer a safe environment for Clare. Now that the investigation was over and the criminals were locked up, he would move back to his own home. There was no reason for Clare to stay here at the ranch—which she loved—any longer

Her dad and brother would be back home by this evening and she could stay with them at the house until her apartment was repaired.

Clare grabbed her robe and threw it on over her sweats and T-shirt before shuffling down the hallway toward the kitchen. Might as well have a cup of coffee before she dressed and packed her stuff and called for a rideshare to take her to the house.

In the kitchen she saw a note stuck to the coffeepot. *"Call me when you're up. Coffee is ready to go, just press the* Brew Now *button. Dylan."*

She got the coffee going and went back to her room for her phone, aware that the nature of Dylan's job meant that he might not be able to pick up her call if he was responding to an incident.

He immediately answered. "Hey, you must be well-rested after that much sleep."

"I am. How about you? It was well after midnight when we got back last night. Must have been hard to get up early and report to work this morning."

The kitchen door swung open and Dylan walked in with a wide smile on his face. "I didn't go into work today."

Delight rippled through Clare as she took in the sight of him in jeans and a T-shirt pulled tight over his muscled arms and chest. She bit her lower lip before finally giving into a wide smile that revealed how she felt. "You took the day off."

They both pocketed their phones.

"I wouldn't say I took the day off, exactly." He shut the door behind him. "I'm out helping Mom and Dad with the horses and in the greenhouse. They want to open the produce stand next weekend." He stepped closer to Clare. "We have some strawberries that are doing spectacularly well."

"Do you?" Clare said in a near whisper. Because while her brain told her he was talking about fruit, the butterflies in her stomach and the blush of her skin spoke to her about something else. Like how much she loved this man and the possibility that he'd been hanging around the ranch waiting to see her because he cared about her in the same way she cared about him. Nerves electrified her skin as she considered the possibility. Did she dare believe it?

Clare had told herself that moving on in life without Dylan was a matter of making the decision and following through on it. But her heart knew better. And those two warring aspects of herself left her frozen in place.

Dylan took a step even closer. His gaze went to the top of Clare's head and a slight smile crossed his lips. Her hand flew up to fix the messy bun that she'd slept on and hadn't thought to fix after she'd gotten up.

The deputy put his hand atop hers, the gentleness of his touch sending her heart skittering. "Leave it like that, please. I like it."

"No, you don't." Clare rolled her eyes and then averted her gaze because right now with him so close and his hand on hers, it all felt like too much. Everything between them felt like too much and her mind was spinning like a top. She'd been foolish to let her emotions get so out of hand, though for the life of her she couldn't figure out when that had started happening.

Dylan dropped his palm from her hair and then reached for her hands, entangling her fingers with his. "That kiss, yesterday…" he said, letting the rest of the sentence trail off.

Okay, they were going to talk about the kiss, apparently. Clare giggled nervously and immediately felt ridiculous.

"The thing is," Dylan began gently, "I *meant* it. And I need to know if you did, too."

Everything within Clare stilled and she locked gazes with him. "If you want to leave town, I don't want to stop you," she said, putting more conviction into the statement than she actually felt. But it had to be said. It wasn't a direct answer to his questions, but in some ways it was more important.

Dylan shook his head. "I don't want to go anywhere unless you're there, too."

Clare blinked several times, trying to figure out what this meant. "I don't want you to stay because of me," she began, realizing that her words probably sounded presumptuous, but right now she didn't care. "Changing your life plans on the possibility of a relationship might not work out well in the long term." And she would not go through what her parents experienced. She would be cautious and smart and prayerful about her decisions.

Dylan reached out and brushed a finger across her jawline, triggering a heavy sigh from Clare.

"I've come to realize that the thing I need to make my life happy and content is *not* just a more intense version of the same things I already have," he said. "Not a more adrenaline-fueled job. What I need is someone by my side, someone I can love and protect and one day build a family with. That's what has been missing from my life, but I didn't realize it until these last few days that I've spent with you. And now I know you are what I need to make my life fulfilling."

Clare gazed into his eyes, savoring the warmth and love and strength she saw there. But then, after a moment his expression became troubled.

"You've said that you wouldn't want to be seriously involved with a man whose job put him in harm's way every day," Dylan added. "And while I no longer plan to do international hostage rescue work, I do plan to continue working at the sheriff's department. I want to continue to do all I can to help people and take criminals off the streets."

A smile formed on Clare's lips. "You've come to understand something about yourself while working along-side me," she said. "Well, I've come to realize something about myself while going through all these harrowing experiences with *you*." She cleared her throat, taking a moment to organize her thoughts. "The world is full of danger and dangerous people. Obviously, I already knew that. I also know I have no desire to face down dangerous criminals. I've had enough of that to last me a lifetime. But I would be proud to share my life with a man who was willing to do exactly that."

Dylan leaned down toward her until his lips hovered just above hers. "I've fallen in love with you and there doesn't seem to be anything I can do about it."

"Don't think you've gone there alone," Clare whispered back. "I'm right there with you."

She rose up slightly on the tips of her toes to close the gap between them and celebrate the moment with a kiss. Dylan wrapped his arms around her, pulling her close, and Clare snuggled into the comfort of his embrace as the kiss continued until her toes curled.

She'd heard his voice over the police radio countless times and she'd seen him in uniform around town now and then, never thinking he could be the man for her. But in this moment she knew without a doubt that they were right for each other, and that her future looked brighter than it had in a long time.

Sixteen months later

"I can't wait to get her started on riding lessons." Dylan glanced toward the fenced meadow where a half dozen horses grazed as he and Clare drove up to the Ruiz ranch house.

Clare laughed softly. "It would probably be wise to wait a few years for that." She looked down at the newborn baby tucked safely in a car seat and rubbed her finger across the little girl's chubby cheek. "Isn't that right, Jessica?"

"I don't hear her agreeing with you," Dylan jokingly muttered.

He parked the truck and then unlatched Jessica's carrier and picked her up. Clare got out and stretched her back, enjoying the view of the property that was now her home. She'd missed it for the last couple of days while she was in the hospital giving birth to Jessica. She glanced at Dylan and enjoyed the sight of her big husband with their tiny daughter as he carried the baby toward the house. When they got to the bottom step, he stopped and waited for Clare to catch up.

The dogs Tommy and Annie loped across the meadow toward them, tails wagging and ears flopping. When the canines drew closer, they slowed and then sniffed curiously at the edge of the baby carrier. Lulu the cat watched from the corner of the porch.

It was good to be home.

Clare and Dylan had gotten married four months after they first declared their feelings for one another. The wedding had been held in a field of flowers planted specially for the occasion here on the Ruiz property. When they'd returned from their honeymoon in the Cayman Islands, they'd set up residence at the ranch. Dylan's parents had asked them to move in after hesitantly mentioning that they weren't quite as young as they used to be and that they could use some help with the animals and the farming.

Clare looked forward to having eager babysitters on hand helping out while she studied for her degree in counseling. Dylan was still employed at the sheriff's department, having accepted a promotion to sergeant based on Sheriff Finley's assurances that he'd still have plenty of time to get into the fray of things and wouldn't end up bogged down in paperwork.

The ranch house door flew open and Sharon Ruiz hurried out. "They're here!" She was followed closely by her husband and Dylan's siblings and their families as everyone came out to make a fuss and see the baby.

"Have you noticed that nobody cares about us anymore?" Dylan asked Clare with a grin as his family cooed at little Jessica.

Clare laughed. "Yes, I have." Her dad and brother should be arriving any minute to join in the celebration dinner that Dylan's parents were hosting.

There were lots of hugs and countless smiles shared as the new parents tried to get into the house, but with everyone impatient to see the baby, the going was slow. And that was all right with Clare.

The murder of her stepmother had left a feeling of hollowness in Clare's life that she'd once assumed would never be filled. And while there was no way Jessica Barlow would ever be replaced, having Dylan and his family envelop Clare in their love and share their zest for life with her had helped a lot.

So had the healing that had come to Clare and her dad and brother following the arrest and eventual conviction and sentencing of Libby Santos, Max Durand, Kirk Madsen and everyone else who'd played a part in Jessica Barlow's murder or the attacks on Clare and Dylan.

Finally making her way across the threshold of the house and claiming a seat near where Dylan had set their daughter's carrier, Clare gave herself a moment to appreciate all that had been added to her life since that initial attack at the park and her taking refuge at the cabin. Jessica's cold case had been solved. Clare and her father and brother had found emotional healing and closure. Clare and Dylan had been brought together, and had fallen in love and gotten married. Now they had their daughter, Jessica.

Good things had come on the heels of some very trying experiences. That seemed to be the predictable rhythm of life. With a glance at her husband and child and the loving, supportive family around them, Clare was certain that they would all make it through whatever challenges life threw at them, together.

* * * * *

If you enjoyed this Big Sky First Responders book by Jenna Night, be sure to pick up the previous books in the series:

Deadly Ranch Hideout
Witness Protection Ambush

Available now from Love Inspired!

Dear Reader,

Thank you for going on the journey with Clare and Dylan and me to untangle the *Unsolved Montana Investigation*.

It can be hard to let things go, and sometimes that's good. There are things that should be remembered or questioned or pondered deeply.

But there are also points in our lives when it's time to let something go. In the case of our story, Dylan needed to let go of the feeling that he had to prove himself worthy of happiness. Clare had to release her fear of falling in love because she didn't think she could face the risk of another loss in her life. By letting go of old emotional roadblocks, both of them made room for something new and exciting.

My hope for you is that if you're carrying a burden and it's time to let it go, through the Grace of God you'll be able to do that.

I invite you to visit my website, JennaNight.com, where you can sign up for my newsletter. You can also keep up with me on my Jenna Night Facebook page. My email address is Jenna@JennaNight.com. I'd love to hear from you!

Jenna Night

Harlequin® Reader Service

Enjoyed your book?

Try the perfect subscription for Romance readers and get more great books like this delivered right to your door.

See why over 10+ million readers have tried Harlequin Reader Service.

Start with a Free Welcome Collection with free books and a gift—valued over $20.

Choose any series in print or ebook. See website for details and order today:

TryReaderService.com/subscriptions

RSBPA2409